ONE BOY AT A TIME

I stared levelly at Jay. "As for your accusation that I'm with Marc just to make you jealous, that is so dumb it isn't even worth the effort to refute it." I gave a slight toss of my head. "Besides, why would I bother?"

"Because you—" Jay stopped in mid-sentence. I thought I knew what he was going to say, that he knew I still loved him. But now he didn't look so sure. I was suddenly reminded of the old Jay, the sweet, wonderful, slightly insecure guy. I'd loved the imperfections almost as much as the perfections.

When I didn't say anything, Jay gave me a forced smile and stood up. And then he was gone, walking back to his team, walking away from me.

Bantam Sweet Dreams Romances
Ask your bookseller for the books you have missed

One Boy at a Time

Diana Gregory

BANTAM BOOKS
TORONTO • NEW YORK • LONDON • SYDNEY • AUCKLAND

RL 6, IL age 11 and up

ONE BOY AT A TIME
A Bantam Book / August 1987

Cover photo by Pat Hill.

ISBN 0-553-26671-3

Published simultaneously in the United States and Canada

*Bantam Books are published by Bantam Books, Inc. Its trademark,
consisting of the words "Bantam Books" and the portrayal of
a rooster, is Registered in U.S. Patent and Trademark Office
and in other countries. Marca Registrada. Bantam Books, Inc.,
666 Fifth Avenue, New York, New York 10103.*

PRINTED IN THE UNITED STATES OF AMERICA

O   0 9 8 7 6 5 4 3 2 1

One Boy at a Time

Chapter One

"It's revolting!" I pushed my microscope away in disgust and leaned on my elbows on the lab table, shooting a brief look across the room at another table where a particular boy I had my eye on sat staring into his microscope. "It is absolutely, positively, totally revolting!"

"What is, Wendy? Did you find something?" Nan, who was sitting across from me, glanced up from her microscope with a hopeful look. "Did you actually find something moving on your slide? There isn't anything on mine except little green blobs that look like deflated balloons. They certainly don't resemble anything *living*."

"Hmmm—what?" I said, my mind still on the boy across the room.

"Well, I think I probably killed whatever might have been there when I put the cover slip on." Nan shook her head ruefully. Her reddish-blond bangs swung away from her forehead, then flopped back down. "Frankly, I don't really think I'm cut out for a career in science."

"Nan, *what* are you talking about?" With an effort I pulled my thoughts away from the boy across the room and focused on my friend.

"Protozoa—I think." She looked confused. "What are *you* talking about?"

"Hmmm. Oh, nothing." I shrugged instead of offering a real explanation. "I guess I was thinking out loud."

Her glance, before she looked back into her microscope, let me know what she thought. I was acting as if some of the extra-thick San Francisco morning fog had gotten to my brain. Still leaning on my elbows, I watched as she twisted the knob on the side to focus better. I heard the soft crunch of glass.

"Darn!"

My mood hadn't changed, but I couldn't help snorting a small giggle. It was probably an emotional release or something. The giggle ended in a noisy hiccup.

Nan looked up. Her eyes met mine, and she frowned. Then the frown smoothed, and she snorted, too.

"Wendy Fong—Nancy Randall!"

Mrs. Sanderson called our names out in a voice only a few decibels lower than one amplified by a bullhorn. Nan and I rolled our eyes at each other and groaned.

"Would one of you care to explain why you are disturbing this classroom?" She cleared her throat and smiled grimly, and I knew one of the zingers she's famous for was coming next. "If you've made a scientific discovery worthy of prolonged discussion, I am certain we would all benefit from it. Please share it with us, before someone from the Nobel committee beats a path to your table."

Nan and I continued to look at each other, both for moral support *and* to avoid looking at Mrs. Sanderson. I could feel my cheeks getting hot from embarrassment. I hate it when a teacher singles you out and makes you feel like an idiot in front of the whole class. At the same time, though, if I kept looking at Nan I was positive I would burst out laughing. Nan had that kind of tight, lemon-sucking look to her lips that meant she was trying not to laugh. I glanced away. The glance brought me in eye contact with the guy I'd been staring at before— Jay Hammond. The giggle that was tickling my throat died abruptly.

He smiled at me.

I did not smile back.

"Girls!" Mrs. Sanderson's voice filled the room. "I'm waiting." Her arms were now folded rigidly across her chest. "Wendy?"

"I'm sorry," I offered in a low voice. It seemed the easiest thing to say.

"To the class, please."

"Sorry," I repeated, this time a bit louder.

"And now you, Nancy?"

"I'm sorry, Mrs. Sanderson." Nan said it with a perfectly straight face. I admired her calm, cool style.

When the rest of the class had gone back to working on their lab assignments, I turned to her and mouthed, "Whew!"

Nan nodded. Then, with her lips barely moving, she added, "Next time you decide to think out loud, Wendy, do it when we're not in Silent Sanderson's class!"

I nodded, watching her as she looked into her eyepiece again. Her nose wrinkled as she remembered that she had ruined her slide. Then she blew out her breath and removed the slide to do it over again.

Maybe I just shouldn't think, period, I thought to myself. The problem was, though, that I couldn't stop thinking. About Jay Hammond, that was.

Lowering my head, I flipped my biology notebook open and poised my pencil over one of the questions. That was for Mrs. Sanderson's benefit—in case she was still watching our table. I scribbled a word, then leaned on my elbow to make it look as though I was thinking. Moments later I turned and looked across the room at Jay.

He was leaning intently over his microscope. A lock of dark blond hair fell across his forehead, and he pushed it back without losing his concentration. I smiled as I noticed the hard set of his jaw. He looked so masculine—so muscular. It had been those muscles that were responsible for our school's winning most of the swim meets since mid-November.

Helping to win those meets had turned Jay into a hero. East City High had never been known as one of San Francisco's leading schools when it came to athletics, but Jay changed that. Unfortunately, Jay changed, too. He was everyone's hero, and he let their attention go to his head. What really did it, though, was that the prettiest, most popular girls were the ones paying most of the attention—absolutely drooling over him at the meets. I was proud at first. I mean, it was kind of a thrill to have someone like Cissy Warner, who's head cheerleader, come over to me and say things like, "You're Jay's girlfriend, aren't you? How lucky can you get!"

But when Jay started to actually believe all the praise people were handing him, I started wondering just how lucky I was. And I began thinking that what I wanted most was to have the old Jay back. The one who thought *he* was lucky because *I* loved him.

I started wishing something magical would happen—he would suddenly wake up one morning, for example, and decide that he hated swimming and didn't want to be on the team anymore.

But of course that didn't happen. And the situation just kept getting worse. It reached a point the last week, when there were so many girls standing around him at the end of the Friday meet that I felt as though I should take a number just to talk to him. And when I finally did, I was so angry that I ended up telling him to go pick up a pair of twenty-pound weights and throw himself back into the deep end of the pool. Then I turned around and marched off, telling myself at the same time that I was never, ever, going to speak to him again.

And I had meant it last week.

I still did—well, mostly.

"Wendy!" Nan hit my elbow. "Wake up! Class is over."

"Huh!" I blinked at her.

"You can put your 'scope away." She smiled.

"We made it. It's almost lunchtime! The bell's about to ring."

"Oh." I frowned a little and stood up and pushed my chair back. Picking up my microscope, I joined the line at the back of the room. I matched the number thirty-nine painted on the arm of my microscope with the thirty-nine painted on the edge of the low cabinet shelf and slid it into place.

Straightening up, I came face to face with my own reflection in the window above the cabinet. It was foggy and gloomy outside, and the overhead lights in the room turned the window into a mirror, except that you could see the trees outside and the buildings across the street.

As I stared at the girl who appeared to be standing just outside the window, I had a kind of *Alice-Through-the-Looking Glass* feeling. My thought was that she'd be pretty if she weren't wearing a slightly grouchy and unhappy look— dark eyes that tilted a little at the corners, short black hair that was wavy with short bangs, high cheekbones, and a mouth that would look better smiling.

But I don't feel like smiling, I thought with determination, about to turn around. Then suddenly there was another reflection, that of a boy coming up to stand behind the girl in the window. He smiled down at her.

Steeling myself, I turned. I looked up, meaning just to tell Jay to move so I could go back to my seat. But then that smile hit me full force, echoed by the warmth in his blue-green eyes. I felt that if I said anything at all at that moment I'd end up betraying how I really just wanted to put my head against his chest and have his arms go around me and hold me tight. So I didn't say anything.

For a long moment I had to remind myself why I was being cool toward him. That reminder put me back in control of myself. "Excuse me," I said very politely but with total reserve. Then I pushed past him as gracefully as possible.

"Well, you certainly chilled him!" Nan commented when I sat back down at our table. "To be honest, I thought you would have crumbled long before this."

"I told you I meant what I said," I replied. I think I sounded a lot firmer than I felt. I started stacking my books, pushing my knees together to stop them from shaking.

Nan knows all about my problem with Jay. She and I have been really good friends for about three years now, ever since her family moved into the house just behind mine. We share a backyard, with just a border of flowers to show where her yard ends and ours begins.

8

We also share our innermost feelings and secrets. There are lots of times when I tell her things I feel too awkward to discuss with my mom. Nan feels the same way. I think it's very important to have a friend who's that close, and I'm glad I've got Nan.

The bell rang finally. Wanting to reach the door before Jay got there, I grabbed my books and leaped up.

But he had already cut across the room to intercept me. He leaned one arm against the wall, successfully blocking my way. I thought about it for a second and then decided just to stand there and wait patiently until he gave up and let me by. This time I refused to look at him.

"Come on, Wendy," Jay said in a light, almost playful tone. "Don't you think you've been upset long enough?" He tipped my chin up with one finger so that I had to meet his eyes.

"Obviously not nearly long enough," I answered. I lowered my lashes, looking at the blur that was his hand. Then I reached up and pushed his hand away. "Now, if you'll kindly step aside and let me pass."

"Look, why don't we have lunch together?"

"What, and ruin my appetite?" I shot back. I'd been trying for sarcasm and I succeeded all too well. Even as I heard my own words, I wished I could take them back. I never wanted to say things like that to Jay.

"Let's go, Wendy," Nan said softly from behind me. I could tell from the way she said it that she knew it was time to rescue me. "If we don't hurry, we'll wind up at the end of the line in the cafeteria, and there'll be nothing left but tuna casserole. It's Friday, remember?"

Jay and I were now exchanging silent looks. The three of us just kept standing there. Nan touched my arm. "Wendy?" Jay glared at her, but she held her ground. Finally he gave a little toss of his head and lowered his arm, stooping to pick up his backpack from the floor at his feet. Then he turned and left the room. I watched him head down the hall. Nan tugged at my arm again.

"All right." I scowled. "I'm coming."

Out in the hall we turned in the other direction toward the cafeteria.

"You know," she said, "we really are going to end up at the back of the line and have to eat the dreaded tuna casserole."

"I don't care," I answered. "I'm not really hungry."

"Well, I am. Let's go get a hot dog at the outdoor snack shack instead. It's not that cold outside, even if it is still foggy."

"All right," I agreed, with an indifferent shrug.

We stopped at our lockers to get jackets and then went downstairs and out to the courtyard where a lot of other kids—who were also obviously not lovers of burned tuna—were milling around. We got in line, bought hot dogs and sodas, and looked around for a place to sit.

The courtyard was a big, open blacktop space with the main building on one side, the auditorium on a second, and the gym on the third. The fourth side faced a small hill that ran down to the parking lot. If you looked beyond it, you could see the San Francisco skyline and the Golden Gate Bridge, which separated the bay from the Pacific Ocean. At least that was what you'd see if the fog hadn't socked everything in. That day, though, the sky was echoing my mood—gray and dismal. It was damp, too, and no one could sit on any of the benches placed around the yard. Instead everyone was huddled in small groups.

When I got up that morning and heard the weather report, I had purposefully worn something bright to offset the gray of the day: chrome-yellow tights, matching high tops, and a loose black-and-white zigzag-patterned top. But I might as well have worn a Hefty bag—my cheerful clothes didn't seem to be able to lift my gloomy mood.

"How about over by the gym?" Nan suggested. "There might be a dry spot under the fire escape where we can lean against the wall."

"Huh-uh. Let's not." I shook my head emphatically. On the other side of that wall was the swimming pool—another reminder of Jay. "How about . . ." I pivoted around to look for another spot and in doing so nearly sloshed my soda all over Josh Brenner who was standing right behind me. "Oops!" I smiled apologetically. "Sorry."

"Hey! Not to worry, Wendy." Josh grinned as he caught my arm to steady me. Josh is good-looking, in a football sort of way. But there it was—sports again! You'd think that was all there was to high school life. "I'm glad I ran into you." The grin flashed again. "Or, rather, that you ran into me."

"Right!" I laughed lightly at his joke.

"Umm—I hear you broke up with Jay Hammond."

"You heard right." I smiled up at him as if breaking up with someone was the easiest thing in the world and I did it every day.

"Well, great!" He thought for a second. "I mean, I'm sorry to hear that. Uh—well, you know what I mean, don't you?"

"Yeah, I know what you mean, Josh." I gave

him another smile, this one a lot sweeter than before. Out of the corner of my eye I saw Nan looking at me, probably wondering why her best friend was acting demented. I'm normally not the type to come on to guys. What she didn't know was that standing only a few feet behind her was Jay. I knew he was watching my conversation with Josh, and I hoped he was getting a real eyeful.

"I guess what I'm trying to get at," Josh said, "is that I was, well—well, I was wondering—" He let go of my arm. "Are you free tonight? I thought maybe we could go to a movie. That is if you'd like to."

"Oh, Josh, that sounds really terrific." I gave him a sad look. "But I can't. I'm busy. But thanks for asking me."

"Yeah, right." Now Josh was looking sad. "Well, maybe some other time, huh?"

"Sure, Josh," I attempted a dazzling smile, more for Jay's benefit. "I guess we'd better find a place to eat before our hot dogs get cold."

Nan didn't say anything to me until we'd reached a spot by the auditorium. I unwrapped my hot dog and was about to take a bite when she asked, "Do you want to explain what that little charade was all about?"

"Just giving Jay a taste of his own medicine."

13

I waved back to where we'd been standing. "He was right behind you."

"Ah." She nodded sagely. "Did he see you?"

"I think so."

"Well?"

I considered. "I think it's fair to say he looked totally shocked."

"Exactly my reaction," Nan said dryly. "I can imagine how he must be feeling now that you are definitely not acting like the Wendy he knows and loves. He'll be racing over here any second."

"Hmmm." I narrowed my eyes, looking into the crowd. Suddenly I didn't feel so triumphant. The impression I made obviously wasn't a lasting one. I nodded my head toward a group of kids. "Just look at that, will you!"

"Where?" she asked. "Oh!" She shook her head, wrinkling her nose at the same time. "Muffy Thomas—the boy-chasing champion of East City High!"

"And it doesn't look like Jay's trying too hard to escape," I answered miserably.

"Look, Wendy"—Nan was very sympathetic—"I know this whole scene is a total bummer. Jay is definitely acting like a jerk. But I honestly think that if you can just be patient for another couple of weeks you'll get him back. Swim season is about over, and then we'll be into baseball and there'll be another hero for the Muffy types to drool over. And without those girls hanging all over him, his head's going to deflate back to normal."

"And I'm supposed to just wait around while all this happens?" I shook my head. "No way." I waved my uneaten hot dog. "What about *my* ego? Doesn't it count for anything?"

"What are you talking about? What's wrong with your ego?" Nan looked amazed. "How about Josh Brenner back there? He was dying to take you out! And he's not exactly Mr. Nerd."

"Hmmm." An idea suddenly began to form in my mind.

"Wendy?"

I didn't answer. I was still thinking.

"Wendy Fong!" Nan grabbed my arm. "Look at me!"

"What?" I asked innocently.

"You're not thinking what I think you're thinking, are you?"

"What do you think I'm thinking?"

"That you're going to use someone like Josh to try to make Jay jealous." She shook her finger at me. "Wendy, that ploy is so ancient Cleopatra was using it!"

I looked at her for a long moment, then sighed. "Oh, I guess you're right. It would be stupid." I frowned. "But I've just got to think of something I can do to bring Jay around."

"Yeah." She gave me a sympathetic glance. "What are you doing tonight, anyway? I know you told Josh you were busy, but I figured that was just an excuse. It's Friday, and you can't just stay home thinking about Jay. Why don't you come to the movies with Kent and me?"

"Thanks," I said, smiling at her thoughtfulness. "But the last thing I'd want to do is be a third wheel on your date."

"I'm not sure if going to the movies with Kent counts as a date," she said with a wry grin. "I think of it more as an exercise in watching him eat."

I smiled—a kind of bittersweet smile—remembering how only two weeks before Jay and I had double-dated to the movies with Nan and Kent. Kent had consumed two buckets of popcorn and two giant soft drinks all by himself. Then, after the show, he claimed he was still hungry, and we'd gone to a fast-food place where he'd eaten a hamburger and a large order of fries.

"So? How about it? We could pick you up around seven."

"No, really—thanks just the same. I really am going to be busy. We're having company."

"Oh? Anyone interesting?"

"Not as far as I'm concerned." I shrugged indifferently. "Just a business friend of my dad's. Remember how I told you his import business

16

is getting too large for him to handle alone and that he was thinking about getting a partner?"

Nan nodded. "Right."

"Well, he's decided on this friend of his from back in college, a man named Stan Chandler. He's been teaching art history at a college in Florida, and maybe he's tired of it or something. My dad called him, and he said he'd love to come into the business. Anyway, he just moved here with his family, so they're coming to dinner." I turned my mouth down. "Which translates into my having to sit around all evening listening to a lot of boring talk about Oriental art and business. Dull, dull, dull!"

"You said he has a family." Nan's eyes sparkled with interest. "Does *that* translate into anyone our age?"

"Yes. He's got a son, Marc."

"How old is he?"

"About a year older than we are, I guess. Maybe seventeen. I think my dad said he's a senior." I thought for a moment. "Yeah, he is. My dad mentioned he'd be going to Berkeley next fall."

"Wendy!" Nan shook her head in disappointment. "I can't believe you! Have you looked up the word dull in the dictionary lately? A seventeen-year-old senior from Florida—he's got to have a fantastic tan—is coming to your house for dinner, and you classify that as a *dull* evening?"

"Nan," I said in a superior tone, "how can you expect me to have any interest in a guy I've never even seen when you know how much I still like Jay?"

"Well, I don't know!" She smiled slyly. "But you might as well give it a try."

Chapter Two

That afternoon I stood at the sink helping my mother get dinner ready. As I peeled the shells off the fresh shrimp she'd bought on her way home from work, I thought about meeting Marc Chandler. I wouldn't exactly make a fantastic impression on him if I smelled like a fish market.

My mom was standing at the worktable in the center of the kitchen, chopping vegetables. She was still wearing her work clothes—pink exercise tights and a leotard with a big pink sweatshirt on top. She teaches aerobics at The Body Boutique. Her long hair was pulled up into a ponytail, which makes her look very young. My mom's pretty, and I'm really proud of her. I just hope I still look that good when *I'm* thirty-six. Sometimes when we're out shopping together people mistake us for sisters, and sometimes when that happens she'll give me a mischievous look as if to say "Shall we?" And we'll pretend that we are. Then we'll giggle together about it as though we're good friends instead of mother and daughter. But she can be serious, too, and strict at times. One thing's for sure, though: I wouldn't trade her for any other mother in the universe.

"Your father's really excited about tonight," she said as she opened a package of dried black mushrooms and put them into a bowl of water to soak.

"Is that why you're going to all the trouble of making Chinese food?" I asked. Normally, because my mother works long hours, dinner is something put into the microwave. That night we were having won ton soup, pork dumplings, lo mein, and stir-fried pork with fun see, which are skinny noodles that puff up when you drop them in hot fat.

"Well, I thought it would be nice," she said, looking up with a smile. "It's been close to sixteen years since your father and Mr. Chandler have seen each other. Pork chops just didn't seem festive enough."

"I guess." I nodded. But then I wrinkled my

nose at the shrimp. Eating them was OK, but cleaning them was really a pain. Feeling like a martyr, I grabbed one and made a cut along the back, then ran it under the water to get the sand vein out and put it in the bowl with the other clean shrimp. "It still seems kind of strange to me that Dad would pick someone for a partner that he hasn't seen for so long."

"Oh, I don't really think it's strange," my mom replied. "They've stayed in touch throughout the years." She put a piece of ginger root on the chopping board and began slicing it into thin pieces. "You don't have to stay physically close to a person to know them."

"I guess not." I thought about Jay. We hadn't been what you would call close since the last week. But I remembered how I'd stared at him across the courtyard at lunch that day when he was standing with Muffy Thomas. I'd known exactly what was going on inside his head. Of course, I could hardly compare that with my dad's friendship with Mr. Chandler. But that was the way my mind seemed to be working those days—anything at all would remind me of Jay.

"How are the shrimp coming?"

"Almost done." I lifted my hand and sniffed my fingers. "But I'm never going to get rid of this horrible smell."

"Sure you are," my mother said cheerfully. "As soon as you've finished here, you can go upstairs and take a nice bubble bath." She paused to look at what I was wearing—the yellow-and-black outfit I'd worn to school—and frowned slightly. "And maybe you could put on something a little less loud. How about that nice blue dress Grandma Fong gave you for Christmas?"

Ugh! I thought. The blue dress wasn't my style at all. My grandma Fong, who usually knows exactly what to give me, had goofed with that dress. It was just too plain. Definitely boring.

"I don't understand why you haven't worn it yet," my mom continued. "It looked so pretty when you tried it on at Christmas."

"Do I have to?"

"I think"—she moved some vegetables onto the cutting board and picked up her cleaver—"so!" This was one of her serious, motherish moments.

I sighed. "OK." I picked up the bowl of shrimp. "Where do you want these?"

"Right there's fine." She glanced up then, giving me a big smile. "Thanks for doing them. You're a love. And for getting the woks out and everything. The table looks absolutely perfect." I had already set the dining room table with our best china and silver and put the flowers my mom had brought home into a shallow crystal bowl for the centerpiece.

"Sure, Mom."

I leaned against the sink for a minute, watching as she expertly attacked the vegetables, transforming them with miraculous speed into various-sized slivers and chunks. I wanted to ask her opinion about my problem with Jay and see what course of action she would suggest. Nan had told me to sit tight and wait it out until Jay was back to normal. But that just seemed so passive. I didn't want to hang around doing absolutely nothing like the pile of veggies next to the chopping board. There had to be another way. Maybe she'd had a problem like this with my dad when they were dating.

I wasn't sure that it was exactly the best time for a mother-daughter talk, though. She had this little frown of concentration on her forehead. She's a perfectionist when it comes to cooking Chinese food. Still, I thought I'd give it a try.

"Mom—"

"Whoops!" Startled, she let the cleaver slip. It hit the board just beyond the tip of her finger. "You surprised me, Wendy!" she said with a little shake of her head. "I thought you'd left."

She gave me an I'm-busy-but-I'm-trying-to-be-patient look. "What is it?"

"Ummm." I looked at her. It was the wrong time to ask her about my problem with Jay. "Nothing really important," I said casually. "It can wait."

"All right, honey." She looked relieved, her cleaver poised over a stalk of bok choy.

"I guess I'll go upstairs."

As I left, I heard the clatter of bok choy being turned into slivers.

Upstairs, I started water in the tub and added about half a bottle of gardenia bubble bath just to make sure the smell of the shrimp really would go away. As the tub filled, I got out of my clothes. Turning off the taps, I slid down into the bubbles and leaned back until they were even with my nose.

It was then that I realized I should have chosen a different scent. Jay liked it when I smelled like gardenia bubble bath. I'd first used it right after we'd started going together at the beginning of the school year. There'd been a dance, and I'd bought the bubble bath so I'd smell special when we were close. Shutting my eyes, I could imagine how we had looked, moving together under the soft lights of the gym that had been decorated to look like a tropical island. The bubble bath had worked. Jay had kissed me and murmured into my ear that he thought I was pretty. His voice had made me feel warm all over. The whole evening had been incredibly romantic. I drew my breath in unhappily with a little sob at the remembrance.

Unfortunately I took in some bubbles at the same time and choked. I sat up quickly, coughing. Bubbles flew left and right. This was ridiculous! I couldn't even take a bath without thinking about Jay.

With a firm shake of my head I told myself I wasn't going to think about Jay again, at least for the rest of the evening. Since it was Friday and he didn't have a meet, he was probably getting ready, right that minute, to go out with Muffy or Cissy or—someone else.

Wendy! Stop it! I told myself sternly. I grabbed the washcloth and started scrubbing, hoping that I could scrub the image of Jay right out of my head.

Despite my good intentions, though, I kept thinking about Jay. I thought about him when I looked into the mirror to put on my makeup. It seemed as though it had been years since biology earlier in the day when I'd seen my reflection in the window and Jay had come up to stand behind me. For just a moment everything had seemed all right again. We belonged together, not apart. Sliding my brush slowly over my hair I stared at myself, feeling terribly alone.

I'd put my brush down and was about to pad over to my closet and get the dress my mother wanted me to put on, the one from my grandma Fong, when there was a knock on my door. Half a second later it opened, and my mom stepped in. She had changed into a cranberry silk dress and done her hair up in a sophisticated twist.

"Hi," she said. "Just wanted to see how you're coming along. Your father's home and is downstairs in the kitchen. He's stir-frying for me so I could come up and change." She glanced at the closet. "You are going to wear the blue dress, aren't you?"

"Yes, Mom." I rolled my eyes. "I said I would. Honestly!"

"Just checking!" She smiled. "Mothers do have to do that you know. It's one of the rules."

I was about to comment on her corniness when the doorbell rang. "That must be the Chandlers now," she said, throwing me one last glance. "Please hurry, Wendy." The door closed behind her, and I could hear her heels clicking away down the hall.

Taking the dress off its padded hanger, I

stepped into it and pulled it up over my hips, then pushed my arms through the long sleeves. Because it was lined in silk, I could tell it had to have been an expensive dress, and the wool was so soft. The color was pretty, too. It was just too bad that it was so plain. I zipped up the back and slipped my feet into my only pair of high heels. Then I hurried back to the dresser to find some earrings that would go better with the dress. Somehow black-and-yellow plastic triangles didn't fit the bill.

It was kind of a shock when I glanced up from my jewelry case to look into the mirror and saw that the dress really didn't look as plain as I'd remembered. I actually looked fairly good in it—older, maybe even more sophisticated.

I stared at myself for a few seconds longer, then raised my hand and touched my hair, pushing it back on one side and tucking it behind my ear. There! I looked—eighteen. Well, almost. I smiled. It was fun seeing myself in a new way, a little like playing dress-up. Except I wasn't playing dress-up—in a year and a half I *would* be eighteen. Suddenly the idea of being eighteen and an adult scared me. I was about to take the dress off and put on something that would make me feel sixteen again, when I heard voices filtering up from downstairs. I was supposed to be hurrying.

So, feeling just a little as though I was pretending to be someone I really wasn't—not yet—I put on my good pearl earrings and headed for the bedroom door. I opened it, took a deep breath, went to the top of the stairs, and walked down them with as much poise as I could manage.

Chapter Three

"And this is my daughter, Wendy." My father had his arm around my shoulders and was proudly introducing me to his friend Stan Chandler and his wife.

"Hello," I said politely. "Welcome to California."

"Thank you, Wendy," they both answered, almost at the same time. Then Mr. Chandler smiled and turned to the tall boy standing beside him. "This is our son, Marc."

"Hi," I said. I was looking up into a pair of smiling gray eyes.

"Hi!" His mouth widened into a smile that went with his eyes. "I hope you're going to welcome me to California, too."

"Of course!" I found myself smiling back at him and meaning it. I know there's no such thing as love at first sight, but I think there is *like* at first sight. "How about welcome to San Francisco?"

"I think I like that even better," he said with an approving nod. "Much more personal."

As he spoke, I couldn't help noticing the rest of him, beyond the eyes and the smile. I had to fight a grin when I thought about what Nan had said earlier—how a seventeen-year-old senior from Florida was going to be anything but dull. She would definitely approve of Marc. He was handsome, in a healthy outdoor way, with thick light brown hair. And his eyes were really more silver than just plain gray, maybe because of the contrast with his tan. With that tan he'd certainly stand out at school.

Suddenly I realized I was just standing there looking at him and it was my turn to say something. I said something pretty original: "So, do you think you're going to like San Francisco?"

"Yeah." He smiled. "I think I like the city already." That was all he said. But the way he said it, and the way he looked at me when he said it, made me think he meant something more. Like what, though? I decided that I must have been imagining it.

My mom broke in and suggested that the Chandlers and my dad go into the living room while she and I brought out something to drink.

"Come on, Wendy," she said, touching my arm to get my attention.

"I'll be right back," I told Marc.

"I'm glad," he said.

I followed my mother into the kitchen. She took a bottle of soda from the refrigerator, as well as a bottle of white wine. She handed me the soda after having poured it into two tall glasses from the cupboard.

"They seem very nice, don't you think?" she said as she inserted a corkscrew into the wine bottle and began twisting it.

"Yes," I said automatically. "Very."

But while I got out ice to put in the soda, I started thinking. I realized that a few seconds before I'd been standing by the front door noticing how cute this guy that I'd just been introduced to was. I dropped an ice cube in a glass thoughtfully. And I hadn't noticed in just a general kind of way, I'd really *noticed*. I had seen how his hair curled at his neckline and in front of his ears, and how his sandy eyebrows were straight, not curved, like two light dashes across his tanned face, and that he had a small cleft in the center of his chin, a little like Michael Douglas. I added a few more cubes. All of that surprised me because since I'd been going out with Jay Hammond I hadn't so much as looked at another guy, much less "noticed" one. *Definitely strange*, I thought, reaching for some more ice.

"Wendy." My mom was talking. "I really think that's enough ice."

"Huh?" I looked down at the glass. I'd added so many cubes that the soda was about to spill over the top. "Oh," I said and fished out a couple of cubes with a spoon.

"And would you take these things into the living room while I finish in here?" She put the wine on a small tray and set it near me.

"Yes, Mom. I know what to do."

"Well, I wasn't sure for a second," she kidded. "If I hadn't stopped you, you might have tried to put the entire ice tray in the glass."

"Honestly, Mom!" I said, raising one eyebrow. I picked up the tray and pushed through the swinging door to the dining room. She was already checking the woks, lifting the lids and poking at the contents.

I was too busy helping my mother after that to think about anything other than getting dinner on the table. There's a lot to do when you're serving a Chinese meal, a lot of last-minute preparations. It's a pain. But the Chandlers seemed to appreciate all the trouble. Mrs. Chandler gave my mom compliments right and left and asked about recipes and where to find an Oriental grocery store.

My mother was gracious and told Mrs. Chandler she'd write everything down. Then she laughed and added, "Next time, though, I'll probably serve my real specialty—corned beef and cabbage."

My dad got into the spirit and made a joke about was her *real* specialty take-out chicken.

"Larry!" she protested.

"I'm teasing, honey." My dad grinned. "Besides I love take-out chicken" He winked. "And you always make those great biscuits to go with it, the ones in that tube you pop and then put in the oven—the ones you say are from scratch."

"Larry!" She was protesting again, but she was also laughing.

I looked over at Mr. and Mrs. Chandler to see how they were taking this, and they seemed to be taking it just fine. I had a feeling our families were going to get along together very well. If they could take my parents' corny kidding, they could take anything.

Mr. Chandler and my dad started talking about business right after that, something about import taxes. My mom turned to Mrs. Chandler again and said, "Larry tells me you've managed to find an apartment in the East City High district. That means Marc will be going to school with Wendy."

"Oh, that's great!" I blurted out. "When do you start?"

"Probably Monday," Mrs. Chandler answered. "I don't want Marc missing any more days of school. He's already missed two weeks."

"I'll be glad to show you around," I offered.

"That would be great," Marc said.

"But first you're going to need some new clothes," Mrs. Chandler said. She turned to my mother. "I thought some of the things we have would do, considering this is California. But it's much colder than I expected it would be."

My mother started talking about the San Francisco weather, which is pretty much the same winter and summer. It's never very cold. But then it's never very hot, either. Even in summer there would be days in a row when it wouldn't get higher than sixty degrees. The conversation turned from the weather to which department stores would be the best to shop in for clothes for all of them. Not exactly stimulating conversation, but I'd already tuned out. I'd started wondering what Jay would think when he saw me on Monday with Marc Chandler.

I was a little worried. Would Jay get the wrong idea? After all, Marc was good-looking. I remembered how I'd felt when I looked across the courtyard and saw Jay with Muffy Thomas. And then I had done that dumb thing and openly flirted with Josh Brenner right under Jay's nose. All I wanted was for Jay to realize why I'd broken up with him—because he was acting like a super-jerk, thinking he was so hot. I didn't want him to think I'd given up on him entirely and was interested in dating someone else. But I just couldn't go up to Jay on Monday and explain what I was really doing with Marc—being nice to a friend of the family. Talking to him like that would be giving in. It would definitely weaken my position. So where did that leave me?

"Wendy." My mother was trying to get my attention. "Honey, please help me clear up so we can bring in dessert."

After dinner we all went back into the living room. I sort of expected that Marc and I would sit together and talk. There really was a lot I wanted to ask him about Florida. It must be an exciting place to live. I wanted to know if it was true that alligators would come right into people's backyards and try to eat their dogs, the way I'd heard, and I wanted to know if he lived near the beach and could go swimming anytime he wanted, and if everyone wore shorts all year.

But what happened was that Marc ended up having this big conversation about art with my dad and Mr. Chandler, and the three of them ended up huddling together at one end of the living room, while I ended up sitting between Mrs. Chandler and my mom and listened to them talk about aerobics classes and the best ways of getting around San Francisco. Which, by the way, is not by car if you've just moved there from a flat state like Florida. San Francisco is a series of steep, steep hills and driving on them can be scary.

I watched while my father went over to the glass case where he kept some of the small pieces of his art collection. He brought out a small jade bowl and handed it to Marc, who took it with absolute reverence. I couldn't believe the way he held it, as if he'd never seen anything as great as that dumb bowl. He turned it around and around in his hands, admiring the carving and the details.

"It's fantastic, Mr. Fong," he finally said. "The Ch'in Dynasty is one of my favorite periods."

"I'm impressed, Marc," my father said. "Few people would recognize the bowl as representative of that dynasty." He took the bowl back and handed it to Mr. Chandler. "Your son has a remarkable eye. You must be very proud."

"Oh, I am," Mr. Chandler said. "He has a fair start on his own collection. Nothing as wonderful as this piece, of course."

What was it I had said to Nan? About how

the evening was probably going to be dull? Well, it looked like I'd been right. Because if there was anything I considered a really dull subject it was Oriental art, and Marc was really hung up on it from what I was hearing. I wouldn't have known a Ch'in from a Chang—if there was such a thing as a Chang. All I knew was that I'd lived with my father's art collection all my life. He was always telling me it was an important part of my heritage and so I should know about it and appreciate it. But to me it was just a collection of bowls and statues that didn't look any different from the tourist stuff they sell down on Grant Avenue in Chinatown. It's not that I wasn't proud of my heritage, but having it constantly pushed down my throat got to me sometimes.

"It would be a beautiful piece even if it weren't Ch'in," Marc was saying now.

My father smiled broadly. I was positive that if Marc didn't already have parents, my father would have offered to adopt him on the spot. I almost expected my father to glance over in my direction and say, "See, Wendy. Some children appreciate and learn from their fathers."

Of course he didn't say that. What he said, though, was almost as bad.

"Tell you what, Marc. I've just had a great thought." He paused long enough to make sure

I was listening, too. "There's an exhibit at the De Young Museum right now which includes several excellent Ch'in pieces. And I'm sure Wendy would be delighted to act as a tour guide for a trip there." Now he was looking directly at me. "How about Sunday, Wendy?"

"Sunday?" I sort of choked out. Honestly, the last thing in the world I wanted to do with my Sunday was to spend it in some stuffy museum. Marc might be cute, but I was also discovering that he had a really boring side, too.

Marc heard the way I had sounded. Who in the living room hadn't? "That's all right, Mr. Fong," he said to my father. "If Sunday isn't convenient for Wendy—"

"Nonsense!" My father narrowed his eyes in this way he had of letting me know, without actually saying anything, that I was being rude. "Wendy, you said yourself this morning at breakfast that you were just going to—as you put it—hang around the house this weekend. Isn't that so?"

Darn, I thought to myself. I *had* grumbled something like that. But I'd only been referring to the fact that because I'd broken up with Jay I didn't have a date for the weekend. "Yes," I admitted. "I did say that."

"Then you're free to go to the museum with Marc?"

"Yes." I smiled at Marc. "I'd love to show you the De Young."

"Good!" My dad said. Beaming, he turned to Marc. "You're really going to enjoy the De Young. I promise."

"I'm sure I will," Marc said. But he gave me a questioning look.

Chapter Four

It was Sunday morning. I sat cross-legged on my unmade bed and stared across the room at my open closet. What was I supposed to wear to a museum? I didn't have any idea.

The last time I visited the De Young was when I was in the sixth grade and my class went there on a field trip. All I could recall was walking down a lot of hushed corridors whose walls were hung with paintings that were too high up for me to see.

Maybe if I simply closed my eyes and pointed . . . then put on whatever my finger decided for me.

I tried it. Closing my eyes, I raised my arm and thrust my forefinger in the direction of the closet. When I opened my eyes, I found I was pointing at my robe. *I really would make an impression if I wore that,* I thought. *Oh, well. So much for that technique.* Sliding off the bed I did grab the robe, but only to head for the shower.

Forty minutes later, dressed in pink flower-print jeans, pink flats, and a plain pink knit top, I headed downstairs to the kitchen to get myself some breakfast.

My mom came in as I was leaning into the refrigerator to reach for the orange juice carton.

" 'Morning, Wendy," she said in a half-sleepy voice. She was wearing her robe, and her hair was kind of messy. She and my dad had gone to the symphony the night before. I guess they'd gotten home late, but I didn't know because I'd gone to sleep early.

"Hi, Mom," I said. "Did you have a good time last night?"

"Hmm—marvelous." She stretched. "I feel positively lazy. Your father and I have decided to spend the morning in bed with the Sunday paper, and I'm just going to make a quick breakfast to take back up." She went to the stove and turned the heat on under the kettle, then took down the canister of tea from the cupboard. "Leave the orange juice out, would you?"

"Oh, I'll pour it for you," I answered, getting out two more juice glasses.

"Thanks, sweetheart." She smiled at me. "You are such a perfect daughter. Did I ever tell you that?"

"Once in a while," I answered with a smile. "Are there any croissants?"

"Yes." She put the orange juice on the white wicker breakfast tray, along with napkins. "I got some yesterday. Look in the cupboard right above you. And since you're being so perfect, you might put a couple on a plate for me and your dad, too."

"I knew there was a reason for that perfect comment," I teased. Getting out the croissants, I took one for myself and bit into it. "Umm—needs jam."

The kettle was beginning to whistle, and my mother crossed to the stove. She picked up the kettle, then paused and looked at me. "You look very pretty this morning."

"You don't think it's too much pink, do you?"

She studied me carefully. "No, I don't. It's dark and gloomy outside, you sort of brighten everything up. Like a camellia bush blossoming in February."

I groaned. "It's a little too early to be so poetic, isn't it, Mom?"

"I suppose." She grinned. "But I'm entitled. You know, you looked nice on Friday night, too." Her eyes twinkled. "Marc Chandler certainly noticed."

"Uh-huh," I said, wrinkling my nose.

"What do you mean by that?" She tipped her head to one side. "I thought I noticed a little chemistry going on between you two at dinner."

"Mom." I gave her a pained expression. "I still like Jay."

"I'm confused. I thought you broke up with him."

"I did," I said. "But I didn't." I explained. "He thinks I have. I'm just trying to teach him a lesson in humility."

"Ah, I see." She nodded. "The old silent treatment."

"Yes," I answered. "The way you deal with Dad sometimes."

"When do I do that?" She pretended to be astounded.

"Lots of times," I said, laughing. "And when *you* do it, it works. Where do you think I got the idea?" I tore a small piece off my croissant, dabbed some strawberry jam on it, and popped it into my mouth. "The only problem is that it doesn't seem to be working with Jay."

"Hmmm." She wrinkled her brow sympathetically. "Maybe you're just not giving it enough time."

"That's kind of what Nan said," I admitted.

"Well—" She was interrupted by the sound of the doorbell. "Oops! I bet that's Marc." She looked down at herself. "And here I am in my robe." She picked up the breakfast tray. "Give me a chance to get upstairs before you answer the door." She moved toward the door, backing against it to push it open. "I'm really sorry about Jay, honey, but try to have a good time, anyway. Marc is a nice boy."

"OK. I'll try," I said. But quite frankly, I didn't think that day was going to be anything but dull.

She had made it upstairs by the time I opened the door. I'd already put on my jacket and picked up my purse, so I was ready to go.

"Hi, Marc," I said, pulling the door shut behind me.

"Hi, Wendy." He stood looking down at me. He seemed even taller now that I didn't have heels on.

I liked the way he was dressed. Casual. He looked great in gray cords, a bulky white turtleneck sweater, and a big, loose dark green Windbreaker. Just right for a gray and misty day.

"Shall we go?" I started down the front steps. Our house was one of those narrow old Victorians that sat all in a row, so that they looked like one really long house with lots of bay windows all at the same level. I thought it was kind of cozy, although other people might call it crowded. I took the lead at the bottom of the steps, turning toward the nearest corner. "I thought we'd take the bus down there. One good thing about San Francisco is that there's lots of public transportation." I was already being the good little tour guide.

"I noticed that yesterday," he said, falling into step beside me. "My mom used it when we went shopping. We've got a rental car, but she's too terrified to drive on these hills."

"A lot of people are," I said reassuringly. "I think it takes a while to get the hang of them."

"A while and a lot of nerve." He laughed. "I'll stick to the bus."

"So, did you just buy what you're wearing?" I asked, trying to keep a conversation going.

"Yeah. Do you think this stuff is OK? The guy at the department store said it's what everyone wears here." He shrugged. "But you know how it is with salesmen. They'll tell you anything."

"You look great," I told him.

"Thanks." He grinned.

I thought about what he'd just asked me. He wasn't looking for a compliment, he'd really wanted my opinion. I'd never had a guy ask me something that honestly before, even if it was just about clothes. Most guys I knew always took it for granted that they looked terrific, even if what they were wearing made them look like something that shouldn't be seen outside of a cage. I also liked the easy way Marc talked about going shopping with his mother, not as if it was something to be embarrassed about, like a lot of guys would feel.

We were nearing Powell, and I could hear the cable cars rumbling up and down the hill.

"Hey!" Marc suddenly halted and turned toward me, catching hold of my shoulders so that I had to stop. The eyes that met mine were warm and friendly. "About going to the museum. I'd really like to see the Ch'in exhibit. But it's not that hard to see it's not on the top of your priority list."

"No—honest!" I insisted, feeling a bit guilty. Had I been that bad?

"Yes—honest!" He nodded, then smiled in a mischievous way. "We don't have to let your dad know we didn't go to the De Young. I can see the exhibit anytime. And actually, dragging someone there who doesn't really want to go would be pretty much of a bore." At the word *bore* I kind of flinched. Marc noticed and laughed. "I knew I was right!" His eyes were sparkling. Standing close to him the way I was then, I noticed that there were little flecks of gold in

47

the gray. "Look, do you know what I'd really love to do?"

"No." I couldn't guess. "What?"

"Ride a cable car."

"You haven't ridden one yet?" I was shocked. "What about yesterday?"

"We took cabs or buses."

"Are you serious?" My eyes widened. "Well, great! That's easy." I paused. "But where do you want to go? I mean, you don't just ride cable cars like they're some kind of ride at Disneyland."

"Hmmm, I don't know." He narrowed his eyes thoughtfully. "It's your city. Why don't you decide?"

"Well," I said, thinking for a moment. "I don't know." Suddenly it seemed as though there were so many places to choose from. "Hmm, let's see. We could go to Fisherman's Wharf, or Ghirardelli Square, or the Embarcadero Plaza. There's also Coit Tower, Aquatic Park—"

"Whoa!" Marc said. "Slow down. That first place—how about that?"

"Fisherman's Wharf?"

"Yeah, that's it. I've always heard it's a fun sort of place."

"OK!" I could hear another cable car coming up Powell, so I grabbed Marc's hand. "Run!" I called.

He didn't question me. We sprinted down to the corner and got to Powell just as the cable car started moving again. The cars always stopped at the intersections to take on passengers and they were open, with a seat facing outward on each side. Next to those seats were tall, vertical handbars you could hold on to. Veteran riders liked them because with one foot on the step below the seats, it was like hanging onto the side of the car. I noticed a space big enough for one person on the seat facing outside, plus an empty bar. "Run!" I called out again, puffing. "Jump on."

With practiced ease, I swung myself up and into a seat between an old man who was reading his paper and a couple who seemed so involved with each other that they barely noticed I'd boarded. Marc then leaped for the step and wrapped one arm around the bar, just as the other people who had gotten on had done.

"Hey!" he said, loud enough so that I could hear him over the clunk of the wheels and the general noise of the traffic around us. "This sure beats Disneyland." He grinned. "Make that Disney World. I'm from Florida." He practically had to yell the last.

I nodded because there wasn't much use in trying to talk anymore. The gripman was clanging his bell as we moved upward toward the peak of the hill. Once up, we would go down again, getting off at the wharf.

Marc was busy looking around. There was plenty to see. After all, as far as I was concerned, San Francisco was the most exciting city in the world. And Powell was one of the busiest streets. The cars beside us also heading uphill were bumper to bumper, sometimes matching the cable car's speed, sometimes falling behind. Occasionally a cabbie would spot someone waving frantically and stop in the middle of the traffic so the would-be passenger could jump in. Then there would be a lot of honking and motorists waving their fists in frustration. And the sidewalks were jammed with people walking quickly, most of them carrying shopping bags or packages from department stores. And at nearly every corner there were flower vendors, their tubs making a bright splash in the gray mist of the day.

I watched Marc's face. He looked like someone who really liked what he was seeing. He already looked as though he belonged. I didn't think he was going to have any problem getting adjusted to East City High, either.

All of a sudden I found myself reexamining my opinion of Marc. On Friday night I had concluded that he was cute but not exactly a barrel of laughs. I'd actually groaned once the day before when I remembered I was going to have to spend Sunday with him. And now it looked as though the day just might turn out to be fun.

It wasn't too long before we reached the wharf. We swung off the car to join the crowd already there.

The wharf was always crowded on weekends, not only with tourists but locals as well. I guess you could call the wharf a tacky place, but I loved it—it was one of my favorite places in all of San Francisco. In the nineteenth century it was the center of the waterfront. Now, though, the old brick buildings have been turned into little arcades, galleries, and miniature malls where you can find just about anything—fresh octopus, giant kites, hippie tie-dye shirts, or T-shirts like the one on a girl who walked past us that said, "I MET A REAL CRAB AT FISHER-MAN'S WHARF."

"So what do you think?" I asked, a bit eagerly. I really hoped he wouldn't turn out to be the kind of person who thought the wharf was tacky.

"I like it!" He looked around. "I really like it!" He looked at me, bending down so he could make himself heard over the noisy crowd. "There's so much going on. In Florida everything is pretty laid back. Here"—he waved one arm—"everything, everyone is so full of—energy. You know what I mean?"

"Yeah!" I grinned, happy at his approval.

"Look, should we start anyplace in particular or just jump in the middle?"

"Anyplace is a good place to start."

"OK." He grabbed my hand and pulled me toward a nearby row of stalls displaying costume jewelry. "Take a deep breath. Here we go!"

We walked up to a stand that from a distance looked as though it was filled with a thousand tiny tropical birds of all colors. When we got up to it, though, we saw instead racks and racks of dyed feather earrings. I had to suppress a giggle as Marc picked one really hideous bright purple pair and held them up to his ears. I usually like bright earrings—but those were just too much. "What do you think?" he asked in a serious tone.

I glanced in a little mirror mounted on one of the bigger racks. "Hmmm." I pretended to actually consider them. "No, I guess not," I said. Then I made the mistake of looking at Marc. The comic expression on his face made me burst out laughing. It had to be pretty obvious to the girl in charge of the stand that I thought the earrings were terrible. Too late I realized that she was wearing a pair just like the purple ones, only they were turquoise. "They're really pretty, though," I said hastily.

"Maybe a different color," Marc suggested, still keeping a straight face.

"No, really!" I shook my head. "I hardly ever wear earrings." Shaking my head made the earrings I had on swing back and forth and jingle.

"So I see," the girl said blandly.

"Give me a little while," Marc told her. "I'll talk her into them." He took my hand and started pulling me away. "Right now we're meeting someone."

"You're horrible!" I said when we were lost in the crowd again.

"Just getting into the spirit of the place," he answered, spreading his arms open in an innocent gesture and somehow managing to look innocent at the same time. "Look, there's a man selling shell necklaces. How about a couple of those?"

"No thanks!" I shook my head, quickly steering him in another direction. "I can imagine what you would do there!"

"I'd be perfectly polite," he said. "But you have to admit those earrings were just asking for it."

"You're right." I thought for a second. "Let's go down this arcade. I remember some little shops that really do have some nice things." I tipped my head to look up at him. "Do you like leather and stuff?"

"Yeah, I do." He paused. "But what's that great smell?" He sniffed. "Crab, fresh steamed crab, right?"

"That's what the wharf is famous for," I said. "That, and sourdough bread."

"Well, I just realized I'm starved. I didn't eat breakfast. What about you?"

"I guess I am, too," I admitted, suddenly feeling a pang of hunger. I'd only had a couple of sips of orange juice and half a skimpy croissant that morning. "And I love crab."

"Then what do you say we get some crab now and do the arcade later?"

Marc and I stood by the vendor's table and watched as he dipped into a huge pot and pulled out a big red crab for each of us. He put them in cardboard containers and added a piece of corn on the cob, then handed us a couple of thick paper napkins as well. We bought a miniature loaf of sourdough bread at the next table, just big enough for two people, and some sodas at another table. Then we took our lunch over to a bench near the edge of the pier where we could sit and eat while looking out over the water and watching the boats come in. Some gulls were hanging around, keeping just out of reach but close enough for handouts.

I guess we were both really hungry because we hardly said a word as we cracked open the crab legs and sucked out the meat. I'd only known Marc for a short time, and normally I would have felt a little uneasy about all the silence between us. It had always been my impression that not keeping up a constant conversation was a bad move when it came to "getting to know" a boy. But I felt as comfortable not talking with Marc as I felt when we were talking. I was the first to break the silence after about ten minutes of munching on crab and sourdough bread.

"I'm curious," I said, wiping my mouth with a napkin. "How come you know so much about Oriental art? I mean, on Friday night you identified that bowl of my dad's. I don't even know which of his things belong to which dynasties, and I live with the stuff! I guess I should know more about it. He's always telling me that, anyway. But I just can't get all that interested." I shook my head to show I didn't understand. "From what my mom told me about your father, he was teaching European art history in Florida."

"I know," Marc said. "You probably think I should be hung up on guys like Monet and Manet." He paused to push his pile of crab legs shells into a neat heap. "You know, I think my interest in Oriental art and jade in particular might have started with this little jade horse my dad gave me for my ninth birthday." He laughed. "Funny how it's some little thing that will set you off on something big. Actually the horse wasn't even real jade, it was one of those imitations you order from the Metropolitan Museum. A copy of a Ming Dynasty piece. But I really liked that horse. There was something about the expression carved on its face. Also, I think it was the first really grown-up present my dad ever gave me, and getting it made me feel grown-up." He smiled sheepishly. "You know what I mean?"

"Yes, I really do," I said. I felt a kind of closeness with Marc from his sharing something that personal. His story almost made *me* feel warmer about Oriental art—almost.

"Anyway, my mom saw how much I liked the horse so she bought me a book on jade. Then my dad got me another piece, this time real jade, but not very expensive. I guess from that point it kind of snowballed. By the time I was fourteen or so I had a pretty good collection. That's when I got my first *real* piece, a white jade dragon. The rest is history."

"Nice history," I said.

"But now, what about you?" He shook his head in a disbelieving way. "I don't understand it. Here you are, surrounded by the neatest things." He leaned his elbows on his knees and looked directly at me. I resisted the urge to pick at a piece of corn I was sure was stuck in my teeth. "I'm talking about your dad's shop, plus all that art around your house. And you're bored with it all." His eyes were locked into mine, as if he were really interested in finding out what made me tick. I didn't think I was such a mystery. "The way you reacted to the idea of going to the De Young gave me the feeling you'd rather go to the dentist."

"It's simple," I said, shrugging and shifting my weight so I could look away without it being obvious that that was what I was doing. His question made me feel just a little uneasy. "I am bored with it all," I said. "Too much is too much! I don't know what else to say." Looking down at what was left of my lunch, I pushed at the edge of the carton now sitting on the bench beside me. "I suppose it's just that I'm tired of having my heritage forced on me by everyone."

"Who is everyone?" Marc's voice was sympathetic.

"My father and my grandmother Fong. See, as far as I'm concerned, I'm American." I turned my head to look at him. "I was born here. My mother was born here, and so was my dad. I'm

57

second generation on one side and about fifth generation on the other."

"Umm—" Marc appeared to be thinking through what I'd just said. "What you're saying is that you're rebelling."

"I don't know," I replied with a frown. "I guess, in a way, maybe I am. I just wish they'd let me decide what's important in my life, instead of *telling* me what is."

Marc looked thoughtful. "I think I see your point," he said in a soft voice a moment later.

We both sank into our own thoughts. Then, just as things were beginning to turn a little too serious, a boat whistle blew about fifteen feet away and made us both jump. Marc's pile of crab legs went skittering all over the place, and the people who were walking by kept stepping on them. We both started laughing, and I heard one woman in the crowd say, "Honestly, these teenagers! You'd think they'd been brought up in a barn!"

We laughed again, mostly at the woman and how dumb it was of her to make that comment when she didn't know the slightest thing about either one of us.

Then we picked up as much of the mess as we could and took it and the rest of our trash over to a barrel marked, "KEEP OUR CITY CLEAN."

"What do you want to do now?" I asked. "We

still have a whole afternoon left for you to play tourist."

"Hmm. That boat whistle gave me an idea. If you want to, that is. I noticed a sign back there that advertised boat trips around the harbor. What do you say—are you game for a sightseeing cruise?"

A few minutes later Marc had bought tickets for us both. Then we boarded a fat red-and-white tour boat along with a crowd of other people. Most of them looked like real tourist types—some with cameras hanging around their necks, others wearing the sort of shirts you buy when you're visiting somewhere. I have to admit I had one of those, a blue sweatshirt with "SKI HEAVENLY VALLEY" printed on the front when I went to Lake Tahoe the year before. When I wasn't in San Francisco I was as much of a tourist as anyone else.

Marc and I found a place near the front of the boat and leaned against the railing. Suddenly I felt a tug of excitement. I hadn't been on one of those rides around the bay since I was a little girl. I almost felt like a tourist doing it for the first time.

The engines started turning over, and we moved slowly away from the pier. A gentle sea breeze began to blow against us, and I inhaled the smell of salt air. Marc looked at me and grinned, then put his arm around me in a friendly way. I moved closer to him. We were two friends off on an adventure together. It was fun.

I realized then that in just an extremely short time I had come to think of Marc as a friend. I considered this fact as we sailed out past Alcatraz Island with the fog blurring the old prison buildings and turning them into a castle. There was a lot to like about Marc, I decided. I liked the way he had been open and honest with me about his feelings, which made me think he was sensitive. And I liked the way he wanted to know about me, too, had really listened to me and seemed to understand how I felt. Which meant he wasn't self-centered.

That made me think of Jay. The big problem in our relationship was that Jay was currently acting very self-centered. What was worse was that he didn't even seem to realize what was going on. He hadn't caught on to the fact that I was upset because of the way he was acting. If only we could talk as openly about the problem as Marc and I had been talking earlier, maybe we could settle our differences and get back together. But I didn't see how that could ever happen. Marc was a friend, and Jay was a boyfriend. I'd never thought of Jay as a friend. He was great looking, smart, had a good sense of humor, and every time I was with him I felt fantastic. But I couldn't imagine confessing my innermost thoughts or insecurities to him. I wouldn't want him to think I was anything less than perfect.

Staring out at the gray waves and the gulls circling overhead, I wondered what would have happened if Jay and I had been friends first, the way Marc and I were.

By the time we got back to my house at the end of the afternoon, I was beginning to feel tired. We stood at the top of my steps.

"I really had fun today," I said.

"So did I, Wendy," Marc replied. He touched my hand. It was the kind of touch that could have been friendly, or it could be the beginning of something else. "You were a great tour guide," he added.

"Maybe I'll consider going into the business," I said, smiling. "You know, 'See Wendy! She knows the best places to get purple feather earrings and crab T-shirts—' "

"And don't forget the old hippie tie-dye shirts," Marc said.

Then we fell silent, and there was an awkward moment because neither of us could think of anything else to say. Then Marc smoothed it over. "I really did enjoy the day, but I guess I'd better get going." He took one step down the stairs. "I'll see you in school tomorrow, OK?"

"Yeah—in school." I nodded. "Yeah!"

"Good night, Wendy."

" 'Night, Marc."

I closed the front door behind me and leaned on it, wanting to savor the day for just a minute longer. As I pushed myself away to go to my room, all of a sudden I realized that I hadn't missed Jay Hammond once during the whole time I'd been with Marc.

Chapter Five

Jay was on my mind the first thing when I woke up the next morning. In bed the night before, I'd gone through my day with Marc thinking about how when we were on the boat I'd concluded that the problem between Jay and me was mainly a lack of communication. Which didn't seem to be a big problem that morning. All we really needed was to sit down and talk openly with each other. When I got to school I'd simply find Jay and suggest we have lunch alone together, somewhere quiet where his groupies wouldn't find us.

The day was one of those blue-and-gold San Francisco specials, when there isn't any morning fog and the sun makes the bay sparkle and the tall buildings shine white. I felt very optimistic about my plan as I walked briskly to school.

As soon as I arrived, I went straight to the courtyard where I was pretty certain I'd find him. I saw him almost immediately, and my optimism took a nose dive. It was almost as if the sun had just gone behind a very dark cloud.

Jay was standing with Muffy Thomas, and he had his arm draped over her shoulders in a disgustingly intimate way. Just as if he'd been in the habit of doing it for years.

Well, I wasn't about to let him see me standing there with my mouth hanging open, gaping at the two of them. Though, frankly, I didn't think Jay would have noticed me if I'd walked right past him wearing bells—he was that engrossed in listening to whatever enchanting things Muffy was saying. I turned around and went back into the main building. I didn't want to talk to anyone, so I headed for the nearest girls' bathroom.

A couple of girls were already there. I pushed into an empty stall and closed the door. I leaned against the green metal wall, trying to pull my thoughts together. I felt as if someone had just punched me in the stomach. And it seemed right then that there must be some truth to the saying about love being painful. The pain in my stomach was strictly from seeing Jay with Muffy.

Yes, I'd been jealous and annoyed enough to break up with him when I got tired of seeing him with a huge group of girls hanging around him. But it was different that time. I'd seen him with Muffy on Friday. And there he was, first thing Monday morning, with her again!

I heard the two girls leave.

Taking a deep breath, I decided to go out and see what I looked like. I hoped it wouldn't be too awful.

But just then the outer door to the hall opened again, and I heard voices—I also heard my name being mentioned. Pulling back, I leaned against the metal wall again and listened.

"But he just broke up with Wendy a few days ago," one of the girls was saying.

"I know. But from what I hear, he moves pretty fast."

"Really? I never heard that about Jay."

"Well, it's true!"

"Can I borrow your comb?"

"Do you have cooties?"

"Yes, of course! Can't you see them crawling out to attack you? No, dummy! Give me your comb!"

"Here."

"Who'd you hear that from? I mean about Jay."

"Well, actually, I suppose I didn't hear it from

anyone. But it's so obvious, don't you think? I mean, I saw him at the movies with Muffy on Friday, then just now in the courtyard he was absolutely hanging all over her. I feel *soooo* sorry for Wendy Fong."

"You feel *sorry* for her! I wish I were so cute. Listen, she can have anybody she wants. Here's your comb back. Can I borrow your gloss?"

"Don't you ever buy anything of your own? Honestly!"

I shifted my weight slightly against the stall wall. It was strange hearing people talk about me like that. I'd never thought about myself as being the kind of girl who could get any guy she wanted. And I'm not, or I'd have Jay. Still . . .

There was the sound of something dropping in the sink and a *"Darn!"*

"Oh, thanks. Now half my gloss is in the sink."

"Sooorrry! Look, you know I think it's Muffy who's the fast worker. She practically cruises the courtyard waiting for couples to split up. Then she pounces—just like a big, fat cat."

"Well, I don't know, maybe we shouldn't be so hard on Muffy," the first girl said. "If I thought I had even the slightest chance I'd probably try moving in on Jay Hammond myself. He is adorable."

"True!" There was the sound of a purse being

zipped up. "Come on, we'd better go. I've still got to get something out of my locker." I heard them start for the door. "By the way, did I tell you about the gorgeous sweater I found at the Clothes Closet?"

I didn't hear any more. The girls were gone. But even if they'd still been yacking right outside my stall, I don't think I would have paid attention. Here I'd been planning how to get back together with Jay, and he'd been taking Muffy out on a date. Tears sprang to my eyes. Seeing him out there in the courtyard talking to her had been bad enough. But imagining the two of them sitting together in a dark theater—it was just too much to bear.

I started thinking angry thoughts about going out and slapping Jay, telling him exactly what I thought. I figured I might as well slap Muffy while I was at it. But those thoughts lasted only a couple of seconds. I'm not the type to slap anyone. More girls came in, and I became practical. Wiping my eyes, I flushed the toilet so it would seem as though I'd been in there for a reason. Then I slipped up the latch, pushed the door open, and walked over to one of the sinks. Without meeting anyone's eyes, I went through the motions of running a brush over my hair and checking my eye makeup. I was especially concerned about the area under my lower lashes, because I might have smeared my mascara.

Once I had collected myself, I went back out to the courtyard. Nan was there, along with some of my other friends. There was Beth Tanner, a tiny blonde who looked more as if she were thirteen than sixteen. And Cindy Layton, who was close to six feet tall and had pale skin and orangy-red hair. Cindy and I spent one summer at camp telling everyone we were sisters, and by the end of our stay we almost had people convinced. Angie Bower was with Nan, too. She's black and very sophisticated-looking, and she wants to be a dress designer. Angie makes all her own clothes, and she's always fabulously dressed.

I walked up to them. They were all talking and didn't see me at first. Then Beth spotted me and nudged Cindy with her elbow. Suddenly everyone stopped talking, and Cindy turned slightly red.

"Oh, hi, Wendy!" she said. "We were just talk— wondering where you were." Her eyes were all sympathy.

"Hey, Wendy!" Nan turned and put her arm around my shoulders to give me a friendly squeeze. "I was beginning to worry that maybe you were sick today."

"No," I said quietly. "I'm fine." I looked around

at my friends. "It's OK, you guys. I know you were talking about me. I saw Jay—and Muffy—earlier, and it wasn't too hard to figure everything out."

There was a genuine sigh of relief from everyone. Then Angie reached out and put her hand on my arm "We were just saying how lousy we think Jay is acting, that's all."

"Umm-hmmm," I mumbled, suddenly afraid I might start crying again.

"He's such a rat!" Cindy added and shot a quick glance across the now-crowded area.

I glanced in the same direction and saw Jay talking to Muffy and one of Muffy's friends.

Jay happened to look over at the same time, and our eyes met. He looked surprised to see me, almost as though he was feeling guilty about what had happened. I just stared back for a moment. Then I turned away, back to my own group, as if he weren't worth looking at any longer.

"Look, let's stop talking about Jay," Nan suggested diplomatically. She turned to me with a smile. "How was your company Friday night? Especially that guy, what did you say his name was? Mike?"

"Marc," I said. "And he's very nice—" All at once I remembered I'd promised to show him around school that day. I wondered if he was there yet. It was getting close to first bell. I considered checking at the main office and leaving a note for him.

"And?" Nan said, prompting.

"He's nice," I repeated, not wanting to take the time to describe him more fully. Dwelling on Marc right at the moment seemed almost an annoyance. I could only think about one guy at a time, and Jay Hammond was taking all my mental space.

"Nice?" Nan shook her head. "Couldn't you be a little more precise? After all, you spent an entire evening with him. Was he tall, short, fat, thin, nerdy, smart—"

"Normal," I answered.

"Oh, that's even better!" She rolled her eyes.

"Nice and normal!" Beth laughed. "He sounds fantastic to me—" Suddenly she stopped talking and stared past my shoulder. "Hey! Talk about guys! Turn around and check out the *very* cute guy who just came out of the main building."

I turned to look. "Oh," I said casually. "That's Marc."

"That's Marc?"

"That's *nice*?"

"That's *normal*?"

"What's he doing here?"

"Is he looking for you?"

"I guess I didn't mention it," I said, "but Marc's coming to school here. He probably just finished enrolling."

"Fantastic!" Beth said in a breathy voice.

"I told him I'd show him around this week, introduce him to kids."

"Lucky you!" Cindy moaned appreciatively.

I raised my arm and waved to get Marc's attention. "Marc! Over here!"

Hearing me, he grinned and started cutting through the crowd of students.

"Hi, Wendy," he said when he reached us. "I'm glad I found you. You didn't forget you were going to show me around, did you?"

"Would I do that?" I smiled up at him. Then I introduced him to my friends, and they acted pretty cool.

"Hi, Marc," Cindy said cheerfully. "Welcome to California."

Beth smiled. "The same goes for me."

"Hello, Marc." Angie sounded very sophisticated. "Welcome to East City High!"

"Thanks," Marc said, pushing his hair away from his eyes.

I noticed how at ease he seemed with my friends, and how self-assured—not overly so, just right. I also observed that he looked very handsome that morning. His dark tan made him look as if he'd just stepped out of a travel ad. I noticed other kids giving him the eye, too. I sort of hoped Jay might be looking in our direction as well.

Marc turned and gave me a grin. "Thanks for the welcome committee," he said. "I appreciate it."

"Of course," I said back. "I was up early this morning organizing it." I smiled up at him, remembering as I did the good time we'd had at the wharf. Some of my unhappiness about Jay was starting to fade.

The first bell rang. Marc gave me a questioning look.

"That's the warning bell," I explained.

"Hey, well, I guess I'd better ask you where to go for my first class." He dug into his pocket and pulled out his class schedule. He turned it so I could see it. "I've got PE first. Can you point me in the right direction?"

"That's easy," I said. "The gym's right over there." I pointed to a building on the far side of the courtyard. "But you have to go clear around to get to the door."

"Guess I'd better get going then. I have to check in with the instructor before class." He stuffed the paper back into his pocket. "See ya later." He gave me a little salute and moved off, heading toward the gym with long strides.

The rest of us split up to go different ways,

but not before Beth gave one long, low wolf whistle.

As Nan and I walked to our first period—English, which we have together—she said wryly, "My family should have company like that." She shook her head in mock disappointment. "I'm your best friend, Wendy. Why didn't you call me and tell me about him?"

"I don't know," I answered lamely. "I suppose I had other things on my mind."

"Yeah. Such as Jay Hammond." She nodded with understanding.

We pushed through the jam at the door to the main building, not talking because it was impossible over all the chattering voices. Halfway up the stairs to the second floor where it was quieter, Nan leaned toward me. "You know, it's too bad that jealousy is such an old trick. Because I think if any guy could make Jay turn green, it would be Marc Chandler!"

Chapter Six

I was opening my locker after sixth period when I felt a tap on my shoulder. Turning around, I saw Marc standing there with a load of books in his arms.

"Oh, hi, Marc," I greeted him. "Where were you during lunch? We looked for you."

"Sorry," he apologized. "I ended up spending the whole period in the counselor's office. They screwed up and gave me two wrong classes, so I had to rearrange my schedule."

"Count on the counselor's office to do something like that," I said sympathetically. "Is everything straightened out now?"

"Yeah. There's only one little problem: I still don't have a locker. They've promised to get me one by the day after tomorrow, though. In the meantime, I guess I'll have to lug these around with me." He hefted the books in his arms. They looked heavy.

"Look," I said. "Would you like to share my locker, until you get your own?" Without waiting for his answer, I turned to my locker and pulled open the door. Then I looked sheepishly at the mess inside. It was crammed three-quarters of the way to the top. "Well, I guess I can offer you the top floor," I said wryly.

He grinned. "I thought you'd never ask." He checked the pile in his arms, kept two books and a spiral notebook, then shoved the rest into my locker. As he did, the stuff inside began to slide. I grabbed what I needed and slammed the door just in time before the whole unstable mess could avalanche onto the floor.

"Now," Marc said, "can I thank you by buying you a Coke and a hamburger?"

"Well—" I hesitated.

"Don't say no. Remember I'm a lonely guy, new in town, and I need emotional support."

I looked into his smiling gray eyes, thinking I should come right out and tell him I was still emotionally involved with Jay, that our breakup was only temporary. Or at least that I *hoped* it was only temporary despite such obstacles as Muffy and Cissy and half the pep team.

"Well?" He leaned slightly toward me, putting

his free hand on the locker beside my head. "What about that promise to show me around this week? I think that ought to include the places where everyone hangs out after school, too. Don't you?"

"Well—" I had promised, hadn't I? I hesitated just a second longer. "All right." I flipped my bangs back and smiled.

"Great!" Lowering his hand, he reached for my books, taking them from me. "Let's go before you change your mind." We walked down the hall to the front door. "Now, where are we going?"

"There are really only two places to go," I said, thinking about which one might be best for Marc to try first. "There's an ice cream place and Jerry's. My group sort of splits between the two. But there's also a fast-food place a couple of blocks away."

"Where do you feel like going?"

"Do you feel like someplace noisy? Or semi-noisy?" We pushed through the door and started down the steps to the sidewalk.

"Which one is semi-noisy?"

"That would be Jerry's."

"Then let's make it Jerry's," he said, quickly adding, "It's not that I don't like noise. I just thought it would be fun to have a chance to talk a little more. I feel as though I just started getting to know you yesterday, and I'd like to get to know you even better."

"Uh—huh," I said. I told myself again that I really should tell him about Jay. But then I was probably reading a lot more into Marc's words than was really there. All he wanted was to get to know me as a friend, not as a potential date. Besides, the idea of spending some more time talking to Marc *was* appealing. I was really beginning to like him a lot. As a friend. So why couldn't he be thinking the same thing? And it would be really rude of me to abandon him at the end of his first day at school. "Me, too," I said warmly. "I mean, I'd like to get to know you better." I laughed, and so did he.

Jerry's was really a little hole-in-the-wall place in an old building that survived the big 1906 earthquake. It's dark, but not gloomy—more cozy. There are ancient wooden booths with high sides in the back, and sitting in them gives you a feeling of privacy. We chose a booth after walking through the front part where some kids were dancing to jukebox music and others were sitting or standing around, talking and drinking and eating. I said hi to several people but didn't stop to really talk.

The waitress came right away and dropped off menus, then left while we made up our minds about what we were going to have.

"Sorry they don't serve crab legs here," I said. "But they do make a pretty good burger."

"That *was* great crab," Marc said. "We'll have to go back soon."

"Uh—yeah." He'd thrown me slightly with his remark. It was innocent enough, but for some reason I wasn't quite sure how to answer. I really didn't consider myself free to go out more than once or twice with a guy other than Jay, even if it was just casual and friendly. I was glad the waitress came back then to take our orders.

"What'll you have, Wendy?" Marc asked.

"I'll take the single burger, fries, and a Coke," I said.

"And I'll have the double swissburger," Marc said, checking the menu one last time. "And fries—and a large orange juice."

The waitress left and Marc said, "Orange juice is big down in Florida." The comment gave me an opening, a chance to steer the conversation away from this getting-to-know-each-other stuff.

"I've been meaning to ask you more about Florida. Does everyone really wear summer clothes all year, and can you really go swimming every day?"

"That's right." He got a faraway look in his eyes. "It was great, and I'm going to miss living there." Then his eyes locked into mine. "But there's a lot to like in San Francisco, too."

His eyes and his words both made me feel a bit flustered. If I'd been talking—or rather flirting—with someone like Josh "Football Star" Brenner, I probably would have batted my eyelashes at that point. Instead I cleverly said, "Well, I like it here, too." I picked up my napkin and took some time to spread it neatly on my lap. I looked up again, and the awkward moment—at least, it had been awkward for me—had passed. I took a sip of water. "I am really curious about Florida, though. Is it like on 'Miami Vice'? The reason I ask is that they film a lot of TV shows here in San Francisco, too, and some of them are pretty faithful to the city, but others are absolutely ridiculous." I wrinkled my nose for emphasis. "Like all those dumb car chases up and down the hills. If they actually did that there'd be dead people strewn all over the place!"

"Yeah." He laughed. "I know what you mean. Well, I'm not an authority on Miami. I've never been there. I lived on the other side of the state. But I guess that show does give you the feeling of Florida. You know, the humidity and the way everyone dresses."

Our burgers came. Marc poured some ketchup on his and took a bite. "You're right," he said a moment later. "They do make great burgers here."

I reached for the salt for my fries.

"I like the girls you introduced me to this morning." He poured more ketchup onto his plate, then dipped the edge of his hamburger into it. "Are they good friends of yours?"

"Mostly." I nodded. "They're my gang, I guess. We've known each other for ages. The girl with the reddish-blond hair, Nan, is my best friend."

"What about—guys?" Marc asked. He studied his hamburger nonchalantly. "Is there anyone special?"

Jay, I thought. *Jay is special.* But he wasn't mine anymore. My heart throbbed with a sense of loss I didn't want to share with anyone. I didn't want to admit that my relationship with Jay might be over, as if just saying it would make it true. "No, no one special," I answered. But even as I said it, I wondered if I sounded convincing. I didn't think so.

Luckily the waitress came back to our table then to see if we needed anything else. I figured I'd steer the conversation to another topic after she left, away from the subject of special guys. I was all set to talk about Oriental art, but the waitress seemed to be hanging around longer than she needed to. Then I realized that she was flirting with Marc, in a very subtle way. He probably didn't even realize it. Well, I could understand. Marc *was* cute.

I remembered Nan having said while we walked to first period English that Marc might be the perfect guy to make Jay jealous. But I also remembered that she'd dismissed that trick as being just about the oldest one in the book. At the time, I'd agreed. But now I thought, if the trick is so old that it doesn't work anymore, then why is it still in the book?

I mean, if a person were really obvious about trying to make a guy jealous, it would look stupid. But if it wasn't obvious. If Jay just happened to draw the wrong conclusion about Marc and me, was that my fault?

I smiled, thinking of the possibilities, and reached for the salt. I sprinkled some on my fries.

"You're going to die of high blood pressure before you're forty if you keep that up," Marc commented with a light laugh.

"W-what?"

"You've salted your fries twice."

"Oh?" I looked down at them with a frown. "Did I? I guess I was thinking."

"About what?" he asked.

"Well I—I was thinking about you."

"Oh!" he said in a surprised tone. "What about me?"

"Don't worry, it was something good." I smiled to reassure him. "Actually, I was thinking about getting you involved in school activities. There's a swim meet this Friday, and it's going to be kind of an exciting one. Would you like to go?"

"Yeah! I'd like that a lot." He smiled. Then a wicked, teasing look came into his eyes. "But only on one condition."

"Uh-oh. I'm afraid to ask," I replied, grinning. "What?"

"Will you go with me to see the Ch'in exhibit at the De Young?"

"Oh!" I groaned. But then I quickly smiled. "OK!" I laughed. "It's a date."

Chapter Seven

Jay caught up with me in the hall the next day. It was between classes, and the hall was noisy with lockers banging and kids talking.

"Wendy!"

He was behind me. I pretended not to hear him and kept on walking.

"Wendy!" He caught my arm, stopping me.

I had to turn around. The touch of his hand on my skin sent a warm tingle shooting up my arm. It was amazing how he could affect me that way when I was so furious with him. But if my new plan was going to work, I couldn't let him see my reaction. I looked up at him, my face expressionless. "Yes?" I said in a very cool tone. My resolve almost crumbled as my eyes met his blue-green ones.

"Wendy, please—" He gave me a pleading look. His voice was low and warm and intimate, so that even though we were in the middle of a busy hall, with kids walking all around us, I felt totally alone with him. "Look, Wendy—can't we make up?" His hand tightened slightly on my arm, just a gentle pressure, and I remembered how nice it used to be to hold that hand and have his arm around my waist. "I know I've been wrong. I should have come after you when you got angry because all those girls were hanging around me."

"Oh, Jay." I smiled at him. That was all I needed to hear. My heart started tapping a happy beat.

"I mean, I should have been more understanding," he went on. "I can see how it would make you jealous."

"Jealous!" I yelped. I stared at him, my mouth open. "Is that what you've been thinking? That I broke up with you because I was *jealous*?" I tossed my head angrily. "Jay! You really are an egotist. A first-class one." He was still holding my arm, and I yanked myself free. I continued to glare at him for a count of ten, then I turned and stormed indignantly down the hall.

Unfortunately I realized, too late, that I was heading in the wrong direction. But there was no way I was going to turn around and walk back past him, and I was pretty sure he was still standing there, watching me. So I pretended I'd done it on purpose and ducked into a nearby girls' bathroom. I leaned against the wall inside, clutching my books to my chest. *One thing's for sure*, I thought to myself with a slight smile, *I'm definitely spending a lot of time in the bathroom these days. Maybe I should think about doing an article for the school paper. I could see the headline*—"Brokenhearted Girl Reviews Restroom Facilities." *I could rate them for comfort and privacy and . . .*

"Hi, Wendy!" A girl from my English class walked past me, pushing open the door to go out into the hall.

"Uh—hi," I mumbled back. Then, realizing I couldn't stay leaning against the wall forever, I heaved a sigh and pushed out after her.

I saw Jay next in biology and successfully managed to ignore him. At lunch, though, I decided to show him just how "un-crushed" with jealousy I was.

I was in the cafeteria sitting at a table with Beth, Cindy, Nan, and Angie. Jay was across the room with some guys from the swim team. He happened to look over in my direction just as Marc came up to our table. Knowing Jay could see, I looked up at Marc and gave him the most dazzling smile I could muster. "Hi, Marc!"

"Hi!" He said to me. "Hi!" he said to the others. His attention came back to me. "Wendy, I need to get something out of the locker before next period. I tried the combination you gave me, but it doesn't seem to work."

"Oh, that happens a lot," I said. "I should have shown you the little trick that makes it easier." At that point I decided to take advantage of the situation and put on a real act for Jay's benefit. I did feel a little funny about what I was going to do, and a little uncomfortable because Marc would probably think I'd gone crazy, but I could explain it to him later. Giving him my most melting look, I cooed, "Why don't I come with you right now and show you how the trick works?" I widened my eyes provocatively. I could already see an expression of confusion growing on Marc's face.

"That's OK—after lunch would be fine," Marc said. "Could you meet me by the locker?"

"Meet you?" I gave a light, trilling laugh. "Why I'd love to meet you, Marc."

"Uh, sure." Marc was backing away then, in the way anyone would if they'd suddenly discovered they were talking to a lunatic. "See you then."

After he'd gone, I turned back to my friends. They were looking at me in almost the same way Marc had been.

"Are you all right?" Beth asked.

"Of course." I nodded, although I was wondering about it myself. I'd just made a public idiot out of myself and involved innocent Marc in my charade. Had it been worth it? I took a chance and glanced in Jay's direction. He was staring very hard at me. It looked like I'd scored the message I'd wanted to get across to him. "No, really"—I looked back at my friends—"I'm just fine."

"Sure!" Angie exchanged a dubious look with Cindy. "Sure you are, Wendy."

Twenty minutes later I was showing Marc the trick that's needed to get my locker open. "See, first you have to stop halfway through the combination, hit the door right up here, then finish the combination." I demonstrated. The locker came open, and Marc took out what he needed. "Marc," I said, stopping him as he was about to thank me and take off. "I guess you must have thought I was acting a little strangely back there in the cafeteria. And, well I'd like to explain."

"Were you acting strangely?" he said politely.

"See, I've been thinking about trying out for the school play. They're holding auditions next week and—uh, I was demonstrating to my friends how I'd handle this one particular role. And that's when you came up to the table. I guess I didn't realize I was still acting when I was talking to you. My friends said something after you'd left."

"Oh, I see," Marc said. But I could tell by his expression, that he didn't really. Probably what he really wanted was to ask if the part I was trying out for was that of a loony. Instead, he said, "Well, you definitely have a talent for acting."

"Thank you," I said, hoping I sounded as though I thought he'd just given me a real compliment.

My greatest concern, as Marc and I parted and I headed toward my own class, was how my act had affected Jay. Had that really been a look of jealousy I'd seen on his face?

I didn't find out until the next day when he stopped me as I was about to go into biology. Nan was with me. She looked at me inquiringly, as if to ask if I wanted her to hang around in case things got sticky.

"It's OK," I told her. "I'll be right in." She went ahead, and I turned to Jay. "Well?"

"Look, maybe I said the wrong thing yesterday when I tried to apologize—"

"Is that what you were doing?" I gave him a look of pretend surprise. I remembered very clearly how patronizing he'd been, saying he understood my being jealous of all those giggling girls hanging all over him. "Humph!"

He frowned. "How come you're being so difficult?"

"Me?" I opened my eyes wide. "Me! Sorry, Jay, the way I see it, you're the one who's being difficult."

"I'm not!" he insisted.

"You are, too!" I insisted back. "And by the way, what about Muffy Thomas?" I accused.

"What about her?" He honestly had the nerve to look innocent and confused, as if he didn't even know who Muffy Thomas was.

"I understand you went to the movies with her last Friday." I crossed my arms and narrowed my eyes.

"Who told you that?"

"The entire school knows about your date," I said. "No one in particular had to tell me."

He winced. "Look, I guess I should have admitted that right away. But, honestly, Wendy, it wasn't a real date. I don't care what kind of rumor you heard."

"Going to the movies with a girl is not a date?" I drummed my fingers on my arms. "If it's not a date, would you please explain what it is?"

"We just went together, that's all." He frowned, apparently realizing I wasn't about to buy such a feeble explanation. "She wanted to see this movie at the Paramount, and so did I," he went on quickly. "She just suggested we go together so we could share a bucket of popcorn."

"Oh!" I groaned, uncrossing my arms and throwing them up in the air. "I don't believe you!" I shook my head. "No, let me rephrase that. I don't believe you expect me to believe that! I think we've said all we have to say right now. I'm going into class before I chalk up another black mark in Mrs. Sanderson's logbook." With that, I tilted my chin into the air and stalked by him. What he didn't see, thankfully, was the way my expression crumbled after I passed him.

Nan noticed, though. She gave me a sympathetic glance as I crossed the room and slid into my chair at the table we shared.

"I don't want to talk about it," I said.

"Good!" She grinned wryly. "Because the last time we discussed Jay in here we both ended up apologizing to Mrs. Sanderson and the class for it." She rolled her eyes.

I nodded, wishing I could smile back because I knew she was only joking to make me feel better. But I couldn't. I was too miserable.

I might as well have had lime Jell-O on the slide beneath my microscope eyepiece because I simply could not concentrate on anything as mundane as single-celled organisms. All I could think about was Jay. I was so aware of his being just across the room from me. But he might as well have been on another planet for all the chance we had of ever getting back together.

All I wanted was the old Jay back, the Jay I knew and loved. But the more I worked at making that happen, the farther apart we seemed to grow. When we'd first started dating, everything was wonderful. He made me feel so special that I would walk around with a happy grin plastered all over my face. I missed the way he held my hands as we stood in the courtyard together during lunch, the way he'd surprise me by slipping my favorite candy bar into my backpack when I wasn't looking so I'd find it when I settled down to do my homework at night, or the times when he'd kind of joke around when we were alone and call me his little flower, pretending to be some smooth, romantic hero.

I sighed deeply. I had to stop thinking about the past. It just made the hurt worse.

Nan heard me sigh. She glanced up with a combination of sympathy and warning in her eyes as if to say, "Don't say anything now, Wendy. We'll talk about it later."

I shook my head to let her know I wouldn't

start blabbing. Talking about it couldn't change things anyway.

By Thursday I'd decided that the one way to get Jay's attention—and maybe get him back—was to use the jealousy ploy. The more I thought about it, the more sense it made. Jay had come to me and tried to make up each time he'd seen me with Marc. I just had to keep at it. The only problem was that I hated using Marc. He was such a nice guy and so easy to be with, and I found myself liking him more and more. And being locker mates, we did run into each other a lot.

I was at my locker thinking about this when Marc came up to stand beside me. I'd already started working on the combination. I paused. He hit the locker. I finished the combination. We looked at each other. "We're a great team," he said and grinned.

"You're right!" I answered with a light laugh. As I looked up at Marc I happened to see Jay coming down the hall. Knowing he couldn't exactly miss seeing the two of us standing so close and laughing, I moved even closer to Marc, as if we were sharing an intimate moment. Beneath my lashes, I watched Jay come to a halt, study us briefly, then turn on his heel and storm away.

As he did, a wave of emotions washed over me. First I was elated because of the effect I'd had on him. Then that elation turned to misery. I hated myself for hurting him. And, as I turned back to look up at Marc, I couldn't help noticing that he had been aware of what was going on. As my eyes connected with his again, I noticed some disappointment in his. Guilt was added to my other feelings. Angry at myself, I turned and gave the locker door an extra sock.

It popped open.

Everything in it slid out in a rain of books, papers, a dissecting kit, a sweater, a drawing pad, an apple, and three rock tapes I'd borrowed from Beth.

"Darn!" I swore.

I bent down.

Marc bent down.

We bumped.

I went sideways.

He went forward.

We ended up on the floor. Together.

"Sorry," he apologized.

"That's OK," I replied, blushing furiously at the same time. We were in a pretty awkward position. His face was about two inches away from mine, and he was bracing himself with an arm on either side of me. For a second I wanted to fade away into an alternate universe or something. I felt like such a clumsy cow for falling all over myself and Marc and ending up in this very unique position. We couldn't have gotten more tangled if we'd been playing Twister. Then I started feeling something else. I could feel Marc's leg touching mine and his breath, warm and smelling like Doublemint, on my face. A tingling feeling started right at the top of my stomach and began to grow in this really quick way so that my fingers and toes were tingling soon, too. I was so surprised that my breath caught in my throat and I kind of gasped.

"Are you OK, Wendy?" Marc asked in a very concerned voice.

I nodded, not trusting my voice.

"Are you sure?"

"Yes—yes," I finally managed to get out.

"Whew!" he breathed out. "For a second there, you had me worried. You looked kind of strange." He shifted one of his arms and helped me to my knees.

"Yeah, I guess I must have," I answered weakly. Not wanting to look directly at him, I did an elaborate job of dusting off the knees and seat of my jeans.

Marc was already busy picking up what had spilled onto the floor. I started helping. By the time we had everything crammed back into the locker and the door securely shut, I felt confident enough to face him again. When I turned around, he gave me a warm smile. "Let me walk you to your next class, OK?"

"Uh—ummm." The gold flecks in his eyes sparkled at me. "OK," I said and smiled back.

Later that afternoon, while I was walking home with Nan, I thought about my experience with Marc. Nan was patient for about two blocks, then she grabbed my arm, halting us both in the middle of the sidewalk. "All right, Wendy, talk. You're obviously deep in thought and obviously not about what you had for lunch. I'm not moving one more step until you either tell me it's none of my business or tell me what's bothering you." She looked into my eyes. "You know I'm your best friend. Maybe I can help."

"Oh, Nan." I sighed. "I guess I honestly do need to talk about it. I'm so confused! I keep moving everything around in my mind looking for places to fit things in, and nothing is making any sense. I think I'm starting to like Marc Chandler."

"That's it?" She shook her head. "I like him, too. What's not to like?" She started walking again.

"No—no!" I said. "You don't understand. I mean *really* like him."

"Ohhh!" She stopped. "You mean *that* kind of like?"

"Now you've got it!"

"Does that mean you're finally going to dump Jay for real?"

"No!" I scowled at her. "I still want Jay back."

"OK, you've managed it—now you've got me confused, too!" She put her hands on her hips. "Let me get this straight. You want Jay as a boyfriend?" I nodded. "But you think you want Marc, too?"

"That's about it."

"Oh, boy!" She raised her eyebrows. "Just when did you start feeling like this about Marc?"

"This afternoon," I said. "When Marc and I were on the floor, I got this warm feeling all over. Nan, I think I was hoping he'd kiss me!"

We'd started crossing Mason Street as I talked and reached the other side when I got to the part about the floor. Nan was about to step up onto the curb but she tripped instead. "What did you say?" She managed to catch her balance. "You were on the floor and you got this warm feeling? What floor? Where? How?"

"Well, it's like this." I filled her in completely, including an elaborate explanation of why the accident happened in the first place.

"Hmmm," was the only comment she made at first. Then a few seconds later she said, "Is that why you made such an idiot of yourself at lunch the other day? Because you were trying to make Jay jealous?"

"Was I really that obvious?" I asked, knowing I had been. I could remember the way I'd acted in complete and total detail.

"Are you serious?" Her eyes widened. "Listen, I was waiting for the men in white coats to show up and haul you away." She stopped talking while we maneuvered our way past a pile of boxes just unloaded from a truck onto the sidewalk. "So, do you think it's working? Is Jay jealous yet?"

"I think so," I said without enthusiasm.

"Well, that's great!"

"Maybe." I frowned. "But he's still acting like Mr. Super Athlete. His ego hasn't deflated the slightest bit! If I made up with him now, we'd probably just end up breaking up again."

"So what are you going to do?"

"I don't know," I sighed deeply.

"How about Marc?"

"I don't know about him, either." I sighed again. I probably sounded pretty melodramatic. "Does it say anywhere that you might end up falling for the *other* guy? The one you use to make the first guy jealous?"

"Look," Nan said. "Don't you think this feeling for Marc might just be a rebound kind of thing? That's what it sounds like to me. You're so upset over Jay, it's natural that your emotions might be confused."

"I don't know," I said. "Oh, Nan, I just don't know anything!" I thought deeply for a few seconds. "Except that I can't forget how great it was when I was going out with Jay. And at the same time I can't stop thinking about how good being with Marc makes me feel now."

"Wendy," Nan said after a few minutes, "all I can say is that I think you've got a real problem. And the only person who can solve it is you."

"Don't I know," I said unhappily. "Don't I know!"

"Well, good luck," she said, patting my shoulder encouragingly.

Chapter Eight

The swim meet was with Muir High. We'd lost the last meet with them, and everyone was talking about how Jay was going to help East City High make a comeback.

The meet was being held in our indoor pool, so we had the advantage. It started almost immediately after school was out on Friday afternoon.

I suggested to Marc that we try to get there early because the bleachers were not all that big, and good seats would be hard to find later on. I also wanted to be where Jay could see me—and Marc. Of course, I didn't tell Marc that.

I like swim meets. They're colorful: with all the swimmers, the lines of flags hanging over the pool, and the bright lane lines. There's lots of noise, too. It's only quiet just before the starting gun goes off for each race. Then everyone starts screaming for their favorites—the individual swimmers as well as the teams. And there's something about how the sound echoes in an indoor pool that makes it seem as if there are about three times as many people doing the yelling. Which means that once the meet really gets going, there's hardly any use trying to talk.

The swim team pep squad had a refreshment booth set up in one corner, near the door. Marc turned to ask me if I wanted something to drink, putting his hand lightly over mine as he did. It was a casual, friendly gesture—no more, no less. I thought how he wouldn't have done that just a few days ago, and it made me realize how far we'd come toward being really comfortable with each other.

"Thanks," I said. "But not now. Maybe later."

"OK," he said easily. "Guess I'll wait until then, too." He looked around with interest. "We're the ones in red, right? I think I recognize a couple of the guys from class."

"Uh-huh." I nodded. "East City High's colors are red and white."

I leaned back against the bleacher seat behind me. Our team was doing warm-up exercises on the deck across from us, and I tried to avoid looking at Jay. But there he was, in the front row. My heart did a triple flip. He had such a great body—slender, with long swimmer's muscles. I must have been staring because Marc spoke up.

"That guy over there—the one you're looking at—is that Jay Hammond?"

"Hmmm—what?" Startled, I swiveled on the bench to look at Marc. "Oh, yes. Why?"

"Oh, I just heard he was the star of the team. That, and someone told me you two used to go out."

"Well, yes." I nearly stumbled over the words. "We did." I shook my head dismissively. "But that was awhile ago." My throat just about closed up saying that, but I tried to sound as casual as possible. *Please, Marc,* I thought, *don't ask me any more about Jay.*

"Is he as good a swimmer as everyone says?"

"Yeah." *Why don't they start the meet? Now!*

"What are his strokes?"

"Uh—back and free. But he's been winning for East City in the individual medley." I decided enough was enough. "*You* must be a good swimmer, too. Did you ever swim competitively?"

"Some." He shrugged. "AAU until I was fourteen."

"So why'd you quit?" I concentrated on his answer, listening attentively with my head turned away from where Jay was doing sit-ups.

"Easy. I got bored with practice. I wanted to do other things."

"Oh? Like what?"

"Well, like scuba diving. It's so much more exciting than swimming around in a pool, and there're a lot of places to do it in Florida. There's spear fishing, too. That's exciting."

"That does sound exciting," I said, intrigued by the new things I was learning about Marc. "Scuba diving is something I've always wanted to do, but I guess I'm a little chicken. You know, all those sharks and icky things down there."

He grinned. "There really aren't that many sharks around. Not if you know where to swim. And you haven't lived until you've encountered one or two icky things, like an octopus. They're really not so bad." I grimaced at that, and his answer was a friendly laugh. "Seriously, an octopus can be a pretty nice guy, and smart, too. They're just shy."

"You're putting me on!"

"Would I do that?" he insisted. "Looks like scuba diving's one more thing we'll have to do together." He leaned close to look into my eyes as he spoke, making me feel as though he were offering me something very special. He touched my hand again, and this time it felt more than casual. The warmth of his fingers seemed to slide all the way up my arm to the back of my neck.

"Uh—" What was the matter with me? Why was I feeling like this when it was Jay . . . where was Jay? I shook my head slightly and pulled back.

"I promise I wouldn't let anything happen to you," Marc was saying. "Of course, you'd have to take a couple of lessons first to make sure you knew what you were doing."

"I think you'd better give me time to think about it," I said, not wanting to commit myself— not wanting him to talk about what we could do together.

"Oh, hey, I'm sorry," Marc said suddenly, apologizing. "I got carried away. But diving can be a real passion. Once you've been down, you have a tendency to want to get everyone else to do it, too."

"Oh, I don't mind. It's just that—"

I was cut off by the loudspeaker, which crackled and then blared out a sound that I knew was a voice only because it was the way all meets begin.

The crowd quieted down and stood up. The

next sound over the loudspeaker was the scratchy noise of the beginning of a record, then the strains of "The Star Spangled Banner" echoed out over the water and the bleachers.

Moments after we were seated again, the starting gun for the first race went off. Eight bodies hit the water simultaneously, and the crowd began cheering.

I cheered, too. I wasn't thinking about Jay, but about my school. I wanted us to win.

After the fourth race, the officials began announcing the scores. We were ahead at first, and everyone screamed with excitement. Then the other team took the lead by three points. That got a smaller cheer, because there were fewer people there from Muir. Finally we pulled ahead again, and we stayed ahead because of Jay.

I couldn't help but feel very proud of him, in spite of our problems. But then my bubble burst when all the girls from the team started hugging him each time he'd climb out of the water after a race.

And—of all the nerve—Muffy Thomas walked over to the benches behind the starting blocks where the team was sitting and gave Jay a cookie she had bought at the refreshment booth. How dare she act like he was *her* boyfriend!

If I hadn't been with Marc, I think I might have gotten up right then and done something—anything—to show Muffy that she was out of line.

Later, halfway through the "free" events, someone hit a lane divider while doing a flip turn, and it broke. As a result, there was a lull in the action while one of the judges and the coach from our team took time out to fix it.

"Would you like that soda now?" Marc asked.

"That sounds terrific," I said, putting my hand to my throat. "I think I could really use one."

"I'll be right back, OK?" Getting up, he edged through a group of kids who were sitting on the deck in front of us.

As Marc left, I glanced around and saw Beth and Cindy sitting at the top of the bleachers just behind me. I waved, and they both waved back. Then a funny look crossed Beth's face, and when I turned around again, I realized why. Jay was making his way over to me.

Panic overwhelmed me. I hadn't planned on anything like this. The last thing I wanted was to have to introduce Marc and Jay to each other. Marc was supposed to be my mystery man. But when I glanced toward the refreshment stand to see if Marc was on his way back yet, I breathed a sigh of relief. He was in a line that looked as though it was going to take awhile.

"Hello, Wendy!" Jay said, crouching down in front of me. His skin was damp, and he had a towel around his neck. Water was dripping off the ends of his hair, which looked more brown than dark blond because it was wet.

"Hello, Jay," I replied, acting very cool.

"I noticed that you were with that guy again."

"You mean Marc?"

"Yeah, whatever his name is."

"His name is Marc Chandler. He's new here."

"Look, I can see what you're trying to pull, Wendy," Jay announced evenly.

"Huh?" My coolness slipped slightly. "I don't know what you're talking about, Jay."

"It's obvious. Really so obvious, Wendy." His eyes had a tight look around them. "And I'm a little bit surprised, because it's such an old number."

"I'm sorry, Jay." I shook my head. "But you've still lost me."

"You're trying to make me jealous, being seen with that clown." He nodded as if to confirm his own statement. "Right?"

"Marc is hardly a clown," I said haughtily. "He used to swim AAU. But he gave it up because it wasn't a challenge any longer." I hoped the slur would make Jay cringe, at least inwardly.

"Is that the line he gave you?"

"Marc doesn't have to give lines." I stared levelly at him. "As for your accusation that I'm with Marc just to make you jealous, that is so dumb it isn't even worth the effort to refute it." I gave a slight toss of my head. "Besides, why would I bother?"

"Because you—" Jay stopped in mid-sentence. I thought I knew what he was going to say, that he knew I still loved him. But now he didn't look so sure. A kind of pain had entered his eyes. My heart wrenched terribly, and it was all I could do not to return his look. I was suddenly reminded of the old Jay, the sweet, wonderful, slightly insecure guy. I'd loved the imperfections almost as much as the perfections.

When I didn't say anything, he gave me a forced smile and stood up. "Well, I can't say it's been fun talking to you, Wendy." He glanced around, then shrugged. "Guess I'd better get back and win another for the old team." And then he was gone, walking back to the team, walking away from me.

Marc came back as I was still watching Jay. "Orange OK?" he asked, sitting down beside me. "That's all that was left." There was something funny about his voice. I pulled my thoughts away from Jay and looked at him. He was watching Jay's retreating figure as well, his eyes slightly narrowed. There was a speculative expression on his face.

I groaned inside. What was *he* thinking? What was anybody thinking? "Orange is fine." I forced a casual smile as I took the paper cup from him. "I love orange."

We ended up winning the meet by fifteen points, but I couldn't provide details, because for the rest of the meet I reflected on my conversation with Jay and on the way Marc had looked when he'd watched him walk away. I focused on the crazy goings-on in my mind, pretty much oblivious of the cheering and shouting around me. The meet ended before I had come to any real conclusions.

Beth and Cindy caught up with us as we were leaving. "Hi, you two," Cindy said. "You guys going for hamburgers?"

"Nan and Kent are around here somewhere," Beth added. "Maybe we could all go together."

"I can't go," I blurted out. The last thing I felt capable of at that moment was going to a place like Jerry's. Jay would be looking at me from across the room—or maybe not looking at me— and he would be surrounded by his groupies. No, I couldn't possibly handle a situation like that. "I promised my mom I'd be home early."

"On Friday?" Cindy's eyes were wide with disbelief as she stared at me.

"You didn't tell me you had to get home early," Marc said.

"Well, I was going to," I insisted. "You see, next week's Chinese New Year and—umm—I'm helping my mom put together something special for my grandmother," I said, embellishing the lie.

"Oh, yeah!" Cindy nodded. "I'd forgotten all about Chinese New Year. It's a really big celebration, isn't it?"

"Really big." I smiled and nodded, glad she'd said something that made my excuse sound a little more credible.

"What are you putting together?" Beth wanted to know.

"It's a surprise!"

"Sure, for your grandmother, but you can tell us." Beth nodded her head. "We won't run over and tell her, honest!"

"Look, I've really got to get going." I put my hand on Marc's arm. "You guys have fun at Jerry's, or wherever," I said, tugging lightly on Marc's arm.

"It's too bad you have to get home so early," he said as we walked down the steps outside. It wasn't quite dark yet, but the street lamps were already on, and fingers of fog were beginning to creep around the corners of the buildings and slither down the middle of the street.

"I should have said something earlier about having to leave right after. I'm sorry," I said, apologizing. And I really was sorry. I hated lying. And now that we were away from the meet and just walking together I realized I hated having to leave Marc's company as well.

"Well, I understand about family traditions."

"Traditions?" I looked at him blankly.

"I just assumed what you're doing for your grandmother has to do with your New Year traditions. I mean, it sounded that way."

"Oh, yeah—right." I nodded emphatically. "You're right." Now I was feeling guilty as well. Why had I included my grandmother in my lie? The only thing I was going to do when I got home was have dinner, maybe flip through the latest issue of *Seventeen*, and then probably stare at my ceiling until I fell asleep.

Marc had his father's car. We stopped on the curb beside it, and I waited while he unlocked the door on the passenger's side. He helped me in, then went around to the driver's side.

As we drove through the streets toward my house, I wanted to hit myself over the head or something. I was being so stupid. Marc and I could have gone anywhere—to Jerry's, then maybe to a movie, even down to the wharf. The wharf is great at night, very exciting—and romantic, too. *Romantic!* What was I thinking?

"You're so quiet," Marc observed.

"I guess I am," I answered. "Probably because I yelled so much at the meet." Which wasn't really true either.

"Yeah, I guess I did, too." There was a long pause. Marc turned up a hill, and I could see the lights of the Mark Hopkins Hotel and the Bank of America Building through the windshield. He turned again. "I had fun at the meet. I'm glad you asked me to come with you."

"I'm glad you came." I struggled to make polite, inane conversation. The easiness that had been between us earlier was gone. I just hoped Marc didn't notice, that he'd accept my lame excuse about why I didn't feel like talking.

We reached my house, and Marc drew up to the curb. He turned off the ignition, then turned in his seat to look at me. I turned, too. His face was lit softly by a nearby street lamp. I couldn't see his eyes, just the strong contours of his cheek and jaw. "Are we still on for Sunday?" he asked in a quiet voice.

"Sunday?" What were we supposed to do on Sunday? Then I remembered—the Ch'in exhibit. Of all things to forget! "Sure we're on," I said brightly.

"Good." He leaned toward me, and I could see his mouth as he grinned. "I was afraid you might have chickened out. You were never exactly wild about the idea."

"I wouldn't do that," I insisted with a shake of my head that dropped my bangs into my eyes. "I'm sure it will be very—stimulating."

Marc laughed. "I think I'd better leave it at that—I know when not to push something. But I honestly think you might find the exhibit interesting, or I wouldn't ask you to go." With that he turned back toward his door and pushed down on the handle. "I'd better see you inside. I don't want to keep you from putting together that surprise for your grandmother."

He came around and opened my door, then helped me out. We walked up the steps and stood by the front door.

Then it happened.

He kissed me.

At first I almost didn't realize what was happening because it was so unexpected. But then I realized how gentle his lips were on mine, and how warm. At the same time I felt the slight tickly scratchiness of his upper lip where he was starting to have to shave. The kiss wasn't a forceful one, just firm and nice. I found myself kissing back before I knew it.

"Good night, Wendy," he said softly. He had been the one to break the kiss. Then he headed down the steps, walking quickly to the car. He gave me a little wave before climbing inside.

I stood watching the red taillights wink as the car went down the street and paused before turning the corner.

He'd kissed me.

I touched my lips lightly with my fingers.

Marc Chandler had kissed me. And now I was more confused than ever.

Chapter Nine

I was still thinking about Marc's kiss at the dinner table a little later.

I had spent most of my afternoon concentrating on getting Jay back. Then when the kiss happened I'd found myself responding. I poked angrily at a green bean. How could I have done that? How could I have kissed Marc when it's Jay I really loved?

The only answer I could come up with was that whether I wanted to admit it or not my relationship with Jay had definitely changed. I'd never actually considered that possibility. I was only concerned with getting us back to the way we'd been before. I hadn't wanted to admit to myself that maybe Jay's change was going to be a permanent one.

I sighed heavily.

"Wendy, is there something wrong with your food?" my mom was asking me.

"Ummm?" Pulled from my thoughts all at once, I glanced down at my plate and noticed that I'd barely touched what was on it—fish sticks, fries, and the beans. "No, Mom." I looked at her meekly. "Sorry. I guess I'm just not very hungry."

She gave me that knowing look mothers get when they think they've figured something out. "Did you eat a lot of junk at the meet?"

"Yes—yes. That's it." I grabbed at the excuse. "So would you be mad if I didn't finish dinner?"

"Frankly," my father said, cocking one eyebrow, "it doesn't look as if you started your dinner." It was his turn to give me a knowing look. "I'd say either East City lost the meet or you're in love again."

"Honestly, Dad!" I put on a pained expression.

"Larry, don't tease," my mom said, coming to my rescue. Then she immediately canceled out any points she'd made with me by her own version of adult diplomacy. "Girls Wendy's age don't want to be teased about falling in love. Sixteen-year-olds take love very seriously." She smiled fondly at me.

"Mom!"

"Now you're being worse than I was," my dad told her good-humoredly. Reaching across the table, he patted my hand. "I'm sorry I teased you, honey. Sometimes we forget that it wasn't so long ago that we were your age. If you don't feel like eating dinner, it's OK." He smiled. "I don't think you'll die of starvation for missing one meal." He glanced at my Mom. "Do you?"

"No," she admitted. "I guess not." As I pushed my chair back and stood up, she added, "Don't forget to scrape your plate and stack it in the dishwasher!"

I was halfway to the kitchen when I had a sudden idea. I'd go ahead and do what I'd told Marc and my friends I was going to do. I turned around. "Mom, do we have any butterscotch chips?"

"What?" She looked at me with a tiny pucker of a frown. "I don't believe you, Wendy! Two seconds ago you weren't hungry enough to eat your dinner, and now you want candy?"

"It's for Grandmother Fong," I explained. "Since it's almost New Year's, and it's traditional to take sweet things to family members, I thought I'd make her some honey bars. You remember, I made them for my party last year and everyone loved them. I thought I'd take them to her tomorrow morning."

"Why, Wendy, how nice of you to think of doing that," my mother said.

119

"Yes," my father agreed. "That's very thoughtful." He smiled.

I could tell, by the look on his face, that he was more than just pleased by my offer. After all, I was doing two very important things: being traditional and doing something nice for his mother. But I really wanted to. Not only do I love my grandmother very much, but I'd decided that she just might be the person I could talk to about my problems with Jay and Marc.

"Actually, I think we do have some butterscotch chips. Look in the cupboard where I keep the flour and sugar."

"Great!" I said, smiling. "Thanks, Mom."

The next morning I packed the cookies into a gold cardboard box that I'd found in the closet where we keep all the gift-wrapping stuff. Then I tied the box with a red ribbon, because gold and red are the two colors that are supposed to bring you good luck. I knew my grandmother would appreciate that touch. She always makes sure to wear her red silk dress on New Year's Day so that she will have luck during the following year.

That year, the New Year's celebration was set for the following Friday. It's on a different day each year, and how it's decided is a little complicated. It's supposed to take place on the first day of the new moon after the sun enters the sign of Aquarius. In San Francisco, everyone in Chinatown celebrated New Year's in a big way. And not just one day, either. People started shopping for family banquets a week before the actual day, so there was a lot of activity in the little shops. And kids were out throwing fire-crackers around—the kind with a whole string of little ones tied together. They go *pop, pop, pop* until you think you've dropped into the middle of a Clint Eastwood movie.

When I walked down Grant Avenue, I could hear them popping all over the place. Some kids on a balcony threw some down at me, and they landed near my feet and started exploding. I ignored them, but I remembered back when I had been their age and used to do the same thing from my grandmother's balcony. I was never really allowed to do it, and was sure my grandmother could have stopped me if she had wanted to. But she always made sure she was busy doing something somewhere else so she could just say she hadn't known what I was doing. My grandmother is one of those rare people who has not forgotten what it's like to be young. At least that was the way she seemed to me. And maybe that was why I sometimes felt more at ease talking with her than I did with my mom.

Grant Avenue was a very touristy street. The streetlights had dragons twined around them, and the buildings were painted mostly in reds, greens, and gilt. There was also a bank that looked like a real pagoda, and there was even a phone booth with Chinese lettering on the outside that translated to "Electric Voice House." I knew because my father translated it for me once.

Whenever I came down there I felt closer to being Chinese than when my father tried to get me interested in my ancestry. I looked around and felt at home in Chinatown, and I could understand why my grandmother didn't want to leave here. Yet at the same time, I was also glad that I lived where I did and that a lot of my friends were Caucasian.

My grandmother lived on a street just off Grant. It wasn't as picturesque as Grant, but enough so that a lot of tourists could usually be found there. Her apartment was on the second floor of an old brick building, over a shop. Ever since my grandfather died four years before, my father has kept trying to get her to move into an apartment closer to us. But she always says no, that if she couldn't live in China, then Chinatown was the next best place. I thought that a tiny bit of her refusing had to do with

Mr. Lum. Mr. Lum had been my grandmother's "boyfriend" for the past two years.

As I turned onto her street I could see the two of them standing just outside the doorway of Mr. Lum's shop. They were both short, and they both had gray hair, so they looked very much alike. My grandmother was just a little shorter, though, and she wore her hair in a bun. She was dressed in a padded jacket that day. A tourist nearby, who was trying not to be too obvious, took a photo of them.

That sort of thing happened all the time. It used to embarrass me when I was younger, and I used to wish that she wouldn't dress the way she did, or speak Chinese in public. But now I don't mind at all. Now I've come to realize that it's important for me to love her for who she is. It doesn't matter what a stranger thinks of her, but what she thinks of herself.

Besides, my grandmother has always one up on the tourists. After they'd gone, she and Mr. Lum would turn to each other and laugh. And Mr. Lum would say, "That makes one more home-movie screen we'll be seen on, Mrs. Fong." And my grandmother would answer, "Yes. We truly are celebrities, Mr. Lum." They were always very formal with each other in public. Every once in a while I wondered what they called each other when they were alone, but they'd never told me, and I would never ask.

As I approached them, my grandmother saw me and waved. The tourist noticed what she was doing and looked in my direction. I guess I must have appeared too normal in jeans and my flowered denim jacket. He looked flustered and pretended to be taking a picture of the front of a shop across the street. Then he hurriedly put the cap back on his lens and walked away.

"Hello, Grandmother," I said, coming up to her and giving her a hug. "I brought you some cookies."

"How delightful." She smiled and hugged me back. Then turning to Mr. Lum, she said, "See what a wonderful granddaughter I have, Mr. Lum. How lucky I am."

"I am already aware of that, Mrs. Fong," he replied. Then he smiled at me. "How are you today, Wendy?"

"I'm fine," I answered politely. "How are you, Mr. Lum?"

"Very good." He made a little bow with his head. "Very good indeed."

"Perhaps, Mr. Lum, we might have tea together. With some of these cookies. But first"—my grandmother turned to me—"I hope you might share some with me, Wendy. And some tea?"

"I'd love that, Grandmother," I said.

After we both had said goodbye to Mr. Lum, we climbed the narrow stairs that led up to her apartment.

She served us tea using the beautiful set I'd loved since I was a little girl. Each porcelain cup was circled with a hand-painted dragon, and each one was different.

My grandmother looked at her cup, tracing the gold-and-red dragon head with the tip of a finger. "Are you looking forward to the *Gum Lung*, Wendy?" She was referring to the dragon parade that started at sunset on New Year's Day. Our Chinatown was famous for its dragon, which was a hundred and fifty feet long and was carried by fifty men hidden under the body of the dragon. There were also bands and gongs and firecrackers going off to announce its arrival. The parade went on for hours because every family hoped it would honor their house and bring them good luck for the next year. Sweets were even put out to tempt the dragon.

But it wasn't the parade I wanted to talk about. I wanted to ask her opinion about Jay and Marc, and I was wondering how to bring it up. To my surprise, she did it for me.

"You should bring your boyfriend. Perhaps you two might want to watch from the balcony with me." She smiled. "Mr. Lum is planning to be here, too."

"Thank you," I said. "I'll come, but I might be alone." And then I launched into the entire story, ending with, "So, by Friday, I might not even have one boyfriend."

"And again, you might have two," my grandmother said with a definite twinkle in her eyes. "Not so bad when you are young."

"I suppose," I said, "if you aren't serious about one of them."

"And you are, correct?" She nodded, now solemn.

"I think so. It's just that I don't know which one."

"Ah! A true dilemma."

"I was hoping you might help me solve it."

"But this is a problem you must solve yourself, Wendy."

"Oh, Grandmother, I just can't." I sighed. "I've really tried! But I can't." I shook my head dismally. "One minute I think about Jay, and I hope he'll go back to being himself again. He'll even say or do something that makes me feel he just might, and I get this little excited spot right here"—I put my hand at the top of my stomach—"thinking that."

"Then it is Jay."

"Well, but then I think about Marc. He's so

nice, and we really get along well together." I knew thinking about him brought a warm expression to my face. "It was almost as though I'd known him for a long time right after we met."

"Then Marc is a friend."

"Yes, and he's more than that." I thought about the kiss and looked down at my cup as a little smile touched my lips.

My grandmother waited until I'd looked back up. Her eyes seemed to hold such wisdom. "I'm wondering, Wendy, with all of this thinking about Jay and Marc, have you ever asked yourself one question—which boy makes you feel best about yourself when you're with him?"

I stared at her for a long moment as the question sank in. "No—no," I shook my head slowly. "I haven't."

"Then"—she paused to smile—"may I suggest that you do?"

She waited for that to sink in, too. Then she said, "And when you decide, you're most welcome to join Mr. Lum and me while we await the arrival of *Gum Lung*." Her eyes twinkled. "I have complete faith that you will make the correct choice. And I look forward to meeting him."

"Thank you, Grandmother," I said, jumping to my feet and crossing over to give her a kiss and a hug. "Thank you so much for your advice. And thank you for being my grandmother."

"Oh, but it was very small advice," she replied. "And you are the one who will have to make the ultimate choice. I have but very little to lose." Still, she seemed pleased to know she was able to help me be happy.

I left shortly after that, thinking about what she'd said while I walked. How did I feel about myself when I was with Jay? How did I feel about myself when I was with Marc?

Chapter Ten

My mom was vacuuming in the living room when I got home. As I came in the front door, she glanced over, then shut off the machine.

"Jay called."

"Jay?"

"Yes." She gave me this curious look. "I thought you two broke up."

"I thought so, too," I replied.

She shook her head. "Well, anyway, he called. And he's coming over."

"He's coming over?" I yelped. "Here? Oh, no! When? Why?"

"He didn't say why," my mom said. "But he did say when he'd come by—"

" 'When he'd come by'?" I echoed shrilly. I started to panic.

"Well, when I told him you weren't here, he asked when I thought you'd be home. I told him, and he said he'd be over then." She glanced at the clock on the mantle. "Which is about twenty minutes from now."

"Oh, Mom, no!" I cried. "But I'm not ready to see him. And I won't be, even in twenty minutes."

"But, honey, you look just fine." She smiled reassuringly. When I continued to look mortified, she defended herself. "He just sounded so anxious. And all I could think about was how, the other day, you told me you wanted to get back together with him." She smiled again. "I think he might even be bringing flowers. He asked if you still liked pink roses."

"Oh, no!" Now I *was* going to panic for sure. How did I really look, anyway? Mothers always say you look great no matter what. I ran my hand through my hair. I obviously didn't have time to wash it. I threw a glance at the clock. Nineteen minutes. Not even enough time for a shower! Makeup? Well, I could at least do that. And my clothes. What should I wear? What was clean?

"Mom!" I shouted as I ran for the stairs. "Could you do me a big favor and not go anywhere until Jay gets here, so you can answer the door and I won't have to come downstairs before I'm finished doing something with myself?"

"Of course. I'll even make sure there are some cold sodas in the refrigerator and chocolate-chip cookies on the kitchen table."

"Thanks, Mom!" I dashed up the stairs, already unbuttoning my blouse.

The doorbell rang just as I was zipping up my purple jeans. I'd decided to be casual. I heard my mom answering the door and Jay's voice as I pulled on a big, loose white sweater. Slipping my feet into purple flats, I reached up and yanked out the hot roller I'd put into my bangs, then trotted over to the mirror to attack my hair with a brush. I looked at myself critically. Semi-OK, I decided. Some plum eye shadow, a tiny spritz of my favorite perfume, and I was ready—well, at least physically—to go down and see Jay.

"Hello," I said casually as I entered the living room. When I saw the bouquet of pink roses he held, my heart felt as if it would melt. But I refroze it by reminding myself that one sweet gesture wasn't enough to make up for all the hurt I'd gone through over him in the past few weeks. "Very pretty flowers." I tried hard to make my voice sound cool and distant.

"They're for you," he said, handing them to me almost awkwardly.

"Thank you," I said and took them just as awkwardly. They really were beautiful. The roses were mixed with baby's breath and they smelled heavenly. I wanted to put them up to my nose and take a deep sniff, but instead I forced myself to continue standing there holding them stiffly.

We stared at each other. Finally Jay suggested, "Do you think we could sit down for a minute and talk?"

"I suppose." I walked over to a chair that faced the couch and sat down, putting the roses on the coffee table.

With a little shrug, he followed me and sat on the edge of the couch.

"Wendy?" He leaned forward, brushing nervously at a wisp of hair that had fallen in his eyes. I bit my lip. "Uh—listen, this is really hard for me. And you're not making it any easier."

"Oh?" I gave him a noncommittal stare and touched my finger to one of the rose petals. I had to tell myself to stay cool and not jump into anything. It was up to Jay to do the talking.

"Look, I came over to admit that I've finally realized what a total jerk I've been since swim team season started. Winning all those races just went to my head. I guess my ego really did get to be a bit much, didn't it?" He frowned to himself. "You don't have to answer that! I know how I was acting."

"Uh—well—" I didn't know what to say. I suddenly realized that something made this scene different from the last few conversations we'd had. I'd been so engrossed in putting on a cool front that I hadn't noticed that ever since I'd come into the living room Jay'd been his old self. He was real again, not a single bit of overblown ego was visible. Now *I* was the one acting like a jerk.

"Wendy, I don't blame you for being this way." He looked contrite. "I deserve anything you want to hand me."

"Well, don't get *too* humble," I said, trying to joke a little and lighten things up. I really didn't want him to think I was entirely mean and unforgiving.

"Yeah, I was on my knees for a minute there, wasn't I?" He gave a hollow laugh. "But seeing you with that guy yesterday really snapped me out of the mood I've been in. It made me realize how you must have felt when I let all those girls hang all over me." He shook his head ruefully. "And I knew they didn't really care about me. They were only doing it because I'd won a couple of races. If I hadn't won, they wouldn't have so much as looked in my direction."

"Oh, I don't know about that!" I said with a smile. Jay had never looked more adorable than he did at that minute. All of a sudden I felt so much affection for him that I had to drop my pose and tell the truth. "Look, you were right about why I was with Marc. I wanted to make you jealous," I admitted softly.

"Really?" The corners of Jay's mouth turned up, and his eyes looked happy.

"Really," I said, nodding. "Uh—hey, would you like something to drink? A soda? Some iced tea?"

He looked over at me. I think he realized we'd reached a point in our conversation where we needed to take a breather. "Sure, yeah." He nodded. "A soda would be great."

"Terrific." I got to my feet. "I'll be right back." I headed for the kitchen, but getting us sodas wasn't the only reason why I'd left the room. I wanted a way to switch from sitting in the chair to sitting next to Jay, without being too obvious.

I came back with two glasses of soda, and two coasters—my parents are really fussy about the surface of the coffee table. I set everything down, then casually lowered myself onto the couch. Not too close to Jay, and yet not too far away.

"So you really wanted to make me jealous, huh?" Jay's mouth split in a real grin this time. "Hey, that's great! That means you still wanted to go with me, even when you were acting so distant and upset."

"Now just hold on a second!" I cried, leaning

away from him. "You're starting to act just the way you were when all those girls were hanging all over you, and I don't like it at all." I shook my head. "You're dead wrong if you think that I wanted to go with you then because I didn't! I absolutely hated the way you were acting."

"But—" He smiled again, somewhat sheepishly. "OK, you're right. I was a first-class jerk, but I won't do it again. Honest. I'm just so relieved that you still like me." He leaned toward me, and his voice became low. "You do still care for me, don't you, Wendy?"

"Of course I do," I answered in a voice that sounded to me as if I was short of breath. Maybe I was. I found myself leaning toward him, too.

"Well," he began, his voice becoming even lower, "I guess what I really mean—" He was looking into my eyes, and I realized I'd forgotten just how blue-green his eyes were. He reached over and lightly touched my shoulder. "I guess what I really mean is that I'm hoping you still love me." Jay slid his other hand around my waist, and he pulled me toward him. "You do, don't you?"

"Jay, no—wait." I put my hands up to keep him from kissing me. I closed my eyes to shut him out. I had to think some more. But then I made the mistake of opening my eyes again, and his face was so close to mine, and part of me wanted him to kiss me more than anything in the world.

"Oh, Jay." I sighed, letting him kiss me. His lips felt just as I'd remembered them. They moved gently on mine, and I responded, slipping my arms up around his neck. He kissed harder, and I wanted to respond even more. But something was missing, something had changed. I realized I didn't feel the way I used to about Jay's kisses. Sadly, I was the one to break away.

"Oh, Jay," I whispered, my throat catching with tears. My heart felt even heavier than it had when we'd first broken up because now I knew it was really over.

Chapter Eleven

Naturally, I still planned to go to the museum with Marc. After all, I had promised—and we were friends.

Since Marc had mentioned that he would have the car again—plus the fact that I felt just a bit insecure about going to a place as classy as the De Young—I decided to wear the same pale blue wool dress that I'd worn the night Marc came to dinner with his parents.

I was even more pleased with my decision when I opened the door and saw Marc standing there in slacks and a good sports coat. He looked very mature and very handsome. I knew we were going to make a good-looking couple as we strolled through those hushed halls.

* * *

"Good afternoon," the guard said pleasantly as we entered the museum a short time later. There were a lot of people walking around or standing in front of the paintings and sculptures, studying them.

Marc paused to look at the brochure he had picked up at the entrance. After a minute he turned back to me. "I think the exhibit we want is down this hall here."

Then he put his hand around my waist to guide me. I'd seen my father do that for my mom when she was all dressed up, but when Marc did it, it made me feel funny. But, at the same time, it kind of felt nice.

We entered a room where the pieces were exhibited in glass cases rather than on the wall. Many of the visitors were Oriental, but a lot weren't. And when I thought about it for a minute, I wondered why I'd expected it to be that way. My father sells art objects, and even though his shop is located near Chinatown, most of his customers are not Oriental.

"A lot of these things look like the stuff my dad has," I told Marc. "I guess maybe I need you to sort of explain what I should be looking for." I smiled sheepishly. "Terrible, isn't it? I honestly can't tell what's valuable and what's not."

"Well, look, why don't we start over here," he suggested, leading me to a nearby case. Inside were a lot of tiny vases so small they were more like miniatures. They were all colors, from deep green, to rose, pure white, gray, and each was beautifully carved.

"They're so pretty," I said sincerely. I pointed to a bowl of translucent gray-and-white modeling. "I think I like that one best."

"I like it, too," Marc said. "You know, it's really wild when you look at something like that and think about how old it is. You kind of wonder how it made it through all those centuries when so many other pieces didn't."

"It is kind of spooky when you think about it that way," I agreed. "I wonder what it was used for?" I pointed to the gray-and-white bowl again. As I did, my hand brushed against his. His eyes met mine, and we exchanged a warm glance.

"It was probably used to hold makeup," Marc said. He moved closer to me. "Probably by some pretty girl who looked a lot like you."

"Oh!" I felt very flattered. "Thank you," I said softly.

"I said it because that's exactly how I can imagine the bowl being used." His eyes sparkled with excitement as he went on to explain. "See, that's the main reason why collecting jade is so much fun. You move into another world when you stop to think about who used the piece, what they felt at the time, whether they were happy or sad."

"Or in love," I added. And as I spoke, I began to understand just a little of what my father had been trying to get me to understand all my life. He'd insisted on using dull words like "heritage" or "ancestry." If only he'd talked about those things the way Marc had talked to me just now, I would have wanted to listen, instead of closing off my mind.

We moved on toward another case as I considered this revelation. Looking down, I spotted a bowl that was very much like the one my father had shown to Marc the night he'd come to dinner with his parents. Excitedly, I pointed it out to Marc.

"Yes." He nodded and then studied it for a moment. "This one is pretty nice. But you know, Wendy, I really think your father's bowl is a much better example of the Ch'in Dynasty."

"You're kidding!" I looked dubious.

"No way!" He shook his head. "Not at all."

"Oh!" I said, breathing the word out softly. Suddenly, I felt very small and mortal. At the same time, however, I could hardly wait to go home and look at the bowl that was sitting on a shelf in the corner cabinet in our living room. And I also understood why Marc had seemed so solemn when my father had shown him the bowl. Now I wanted a chance to look at it, too. And, what was even stranger, I wanted to tell my father how I felt.

Perhaps Marc understood how I was feeling. We had nearly reached the last case in the exhibit, and he took my hand as we walked thoughtfully from the room.

A few moments later Marc spoke. "In keeping with the mood, I understand there's a Japanese teahouse somewhere near here."

"There sure is," I said. "We can even walk there. And there's a formal Japanese garden, too, which is really beautiful."

"Then let's go." He smiled down at me, and we quickened out steps, leaving the reverent feeling almost completely behind us in the Ch'in Exhibit room. Almost, but not quite.

We walked through the gardens first. There were arched footbridges that were reflected in the water, making a perfect circle. And there were cherry trees, which would be in bloom soon, and bonsai gardens that were like little miniature worlds, and a ten-foot-high bronze Buddha that had turned a pretty, soft green with age. We stopped by one of the ponds nearby and watched as the large goldfish swam lazily around.

"I like the gardens best when it's foggy," I said, almost adding that it was more romantic when the mist was curling through the trees and around the pagoda.

"I can imagine. But it's also nice now." Marc

smiled. "And I think that Buddha over there likes the sun as well. See, he's smiling."

"Is that really a smile?" I asked. "I can't tell."

"Sure!" Marc said with a laugh. "Well, actually, I don't know. It is kind of hard to tell," he admitted. There was a pause, and in that small moment, I suddenly felt very happy. I wanted to hold on to that feeling, to put it in a special place in my mind so that I could remember it when I was old, and most of my life was behind me. "Do you want to go to the teahouse now?" Marc asked.

"Yes." I smiled up at him. "Let's."

At the teahouse, we were served jasmine tea and small cakes by a middle-aged Japanese woman, who was dressed in a kimono.

When she left, I picked up my cup. "You know," I said, "It's kind of funny. Last week I was your tour guide. And this week you've been mine." I was referring to the things he had told me while we were looking at the jade exhibit. "You're a very good tour guide, by the way."

"And so are you," he said back. "You gave me a terrific introduction to San Francisco. You really made me glad that we moved here."

"Well," I paused, thinking about whether I should confess how I had dreaded spending the day with him at first. Instead, I told him something else I remembered. "When we were riding the cable car, I looked at you and decided you were the kind of guy who would fit in right away."

"Is that what you thought?" He gave me this rueful look. "You know what I was thinking?" I shook my head. "I was thinking you hated me because I had ruined your day."

I blushed. "All right," I admitted. "I guess I felt that way at first. But then, when you said we didn't have to go to the museum, I started to like you." All at once I stopped talking, realizing what I'd just said. "But that was last week," I went on hurriedly. "I really did enjoy seeing the exhibit with you today."

"I know," he said. "I could tell." Picking up his cup, he started to sip from it, then set it down instead. "I guess I can make a confession now, too. I was feeling a little guilty, making you come with me the way I did. I knew about you and Jay, and that you'd broken up. I was hoping it was over, but sometimes, the way you look at him, I wasn't so sure. And I didn't want to intrude if you were going to get back together with him. But if you weren't"—his eyes looked deeply into mine, and I held my breath—"then I wanted to be there for you." He laughed. "I figured if I could keep you to your promise about seeing the exhibit with me, this just might turn out to be our first real date."

A date! He thought of it as a date. A little shock passed through me, but it was a nice tingly shock.

"And to be really honest, I was hoping you'd like the Ch'in jade. See, I love it so much that I want you to like it, too." He grinned at me and spread his hands wide. "You found me out."

"And I really do like it." I paused. "Marc, I have another confession, too." And then I told him about how he'd figured in my plot to get Jay jealous. I knew I was taking a big chance in doing it, a chance that we'd never go out on a second date because he would be so angry and disappointed about what I'd done. But I knew I had to. I never wanted another awful secret between us. From then on, I wanted our relationship to be as open and honest as it had first started out being.

"So if you want to consider this our last date, I'll understand why," I finished. "But I hope that's not what you'll say." I waited for his response, my eyes wide in expectation.

He was silent for a long moment, staring down at his cup and swirling the tea around slowly. At last he put the cup down and looked up at me. "Thanks, Wendy. Thanks for being straight with me." His voice was low, and there was a cloud across the eyes that were usually so sunny and clear. I could tell I'd hurt him.

"Uh-huh," I said, becoming unhappy, too. It was the end for us. But even if I thought I could change things by taking back my confession, I wouldn't have. And the reason was that I considered Marc a friend, not just a boyfriend. A friend who deserved the best from me, a friend too special to play games with. "I guess you'd like to go now," I said glumly.

"Not unless you want to," he said. "And you've already told me you don't." He reached across the table to take my hand. "Wendy, a lot of relationships have trouble getting over a few rough spots at first. But once you're over them, sometimes those relationships turn out to be the best kind. I think we've just gotten past our roughest one." His face didn't have an unhappy look any longer. "So why don't we discuss our second date?" He squeezed my hand, and the corners of his mouth turned up in a mischievous grin. "I think it's your turn to choose."

"Terrific!" I answered, feeling warm and happy all over. I grinned back. "I know just where I want to take you."

Chapter Twelve

We stood on the sidewalk in a soft pool of light from the dragon street lamp above our heads. Marc had his arm around my waist, and I was huddled against him. The night was cool, and we were both wearing warm jackets. I was also wearing a red sweater—for luck.

People were beginning to line the street on either side of us, talking and looking hopefully toward the band, gongs, and distant firecrackers. It wouldn't be long before the dragon appeared, and I was beginning to feel very excited.

"I like your grandmother," Marc said, leaning down so I could hear him over the noisy crowd. "And Mr. Lum."

"I'm glad," I replied. Smiling, I looked up at him. I could barely see his face in the dim light.

"She likes you, too. She whispered that to me just before we left the apartment to come down here to the street." What I didn't add was that she said she thought Marc and I made as perfect a couple as she and Mr. Lum. Marc and I had gotten a lot closer since last Sunday, but I still didn't consider us a couple yet.

Mr. Lum had left sweets at the front of his shop door as an offering for the dragon, and my grandmother had given me a small basket of sweets and coins to leave at the bottom of the stairs, hoping the dragon would see them and acknowledge them. That way they were sure they would have good luck and prosperity in the coming year. I knew they were both on the balcony above us, waiting to see what *Gum Lung* would do.

"There it is! There it is!" I heard someone call from down toward the end of the block.

"*Gum Lung!*"

"*Gum Lung!*"

I gave an excited little hop and leaned to look at it along with the others.

Then I saw the dragon, the head coming around the corner, the body shaking along behind. It came closer and closer until the gongs were almost deafening. Firecrackers started going off in the street and the smell, like hundreds of matches being struck at once, hung in the air along with small puffs of white smoke. The huge gold-and-red head of the dragon looked fierce. It was being shaken by the dancer inside, so that the shaggy fringe and silk streamers flew around it. The hundred-and-fifty-foot-long dragon's body glowed from the light of the lanterns that were being carried inside. It wove from side to side as it came down the street toward us, pausing at a doorway here and there.

"I hope it stops here long enough to see my grandmother's and Mr. Lum's offerings," I called up to Marc.

He nodded. Then he tightened his hold on my waist, protectively pulling me in against his side, as the people around us suddenly began to surge farther out into the street to get closer to *Gum Lung.*

When the dragon was directly in front of us, the head turned in our direction and the dancer inside shook it ferociously at us. It was only for a second, then the dragon moved on, winding its way down the street.

The people around us were moving, too, either along with the dragon or back to where they'd come from. As they did, it was as if we became an island, standing together with no one noticing we were there.

Marc turned to face me. Slipping his hands

around my waist, he pulled me close. I looked up into his face. His eyes were shadowed, but it was as if I could see them, gray-gold, looking into mine.

"Happy New Year, Wendy," he said, loud enough so that only I could hear.

"Happy New Year, Marc," I replied.

A warm feeling washed over me, and I wanted Marc to kiss me. He did, leaning down and ever so gently touching his lips to mine. He pulled away and kissed my forehead. Then, as I leaned my head against his shoulder, he whispered, "I love you, Wendy Fong."

I smiled and closed my eyes, looking forward to the new year—with Marc.

The Spectacular New Series from Bantam Books!

Meet the cast of the sensational fictional soap opera ALL THAT GLITTERS ... beautiful Katie Nolan, dreamy Mitch Callahan, exotic Shana Bradbury. Share the joy and the tears, the glory and the heartache with these young stars as they balance acting careers with the ups and downs of teenage life.

MAGIC TIME: ALL THAT GLITTERS #1—coming in October!
And stay tuned for TAKE TWO: ALL THAT GLITTERS #2, coming in November!

And that's not all ...
Enter the Exciting ALL THAT GLITTERS Contest!
Look for details in MAGIC TIME, but don't delay—prizes are limited!

ALL THAT GLITTERS

Where life is a soap opera—on and off the stage!

FIRST THERE WAS LOVE, AND THEN THE PROMISE
Now join *Caitlin* in FOREVER . . .

In DREAMS OF FOREVER, Book One of the FOREVER TRILOGY, Caitlin and Jed are in New York City. It's summertime and Caitlin is pursuing a career in journalism and Jed is starting law school. After a death in his family Caitlin finds it increasingly difficult to communicate with him. Her new friendship with a handsome photographer is comforting, until it begins to become something more than friendship. Can her love for Jed overcome these upheavals and truly last forever?

Don't miss Caitlin in DREAMS OF FOREVER Book I coming in September, and FOREVER AND ALWAYS Book II coming in October.

While you're waiting for the FOREVER TRILOGY, have you read:

Special Offer
Buy a Bantam Book
for only 50¢.

Now you can order the exciting books you've been wanting to read straight from Bantam's latest listing of hundreds of titles. *And* this special offer gives you the opportunity to purchase a Bantam book for only 50¢. Here's how:

By ordering any five books at the regular price per order, you can also choose any other single book listed (up to $4.95 value) for only 50¢. Some restrictions do apply, so for further details send for Bantam's listing of titles today.

Just send us your name and address and we'll send you Bantam Book's SHOP AT HOME CATALOG!